A
Harlequin
Romance

WELCOME

TO THE WONDERFUL WORLD

of Harlequin Romances!

Interesting, informative and entertaining,
each Harlequin Romance portrays an appealing
love story. Harlequin Romances take you
to faraway places — places with real people
facing real love situations — and
you become part of their story.

As publishers of Harlequin Romances, we're extremely
proud of our books (we've been publishing
them since 1954). We're proud also that Harlequin
Romances are North America's most-read
paperback romances.

Eight new titles are released every month and are
sold at nearly all book-selling stores across
Canada and the United States.

A free catalogue listing all available Harlequin Romances
can be yours by writing to the

HARLEQUIN READER SERVICE,
M.P.O. Box 707, Niagara Falls, N.Y. 14302.
Canadian address: Stratford, Ontario, Canada.

or use order coupon at back of book.

We sincerely hope you enjoy reading
this Harlequin Romance.

Yours truly,

THE PUBLISHERS
    Harlequin Romances

THE TREES OF TARRENTALL

by

LINDEN GRIERSON

HARLEQUIN BOOKS   TORONTO
WINNIPEG

Original hard cover edition published in 1973
by Mills & Boon Limited.

© Linden Grierson 1973

SBN 373-01791-X

Harlequin edition published June 1974

Printed in Canada

CHAPTER 1

CAREFULLY and quietly the girl closed the office door behind her, and as it clicked into position she started to walk along the long corridor with the numerous identical doors which hid behind them the same type of offices as the one she had just left. Inside they would all be the same dimension, the same height and with the same quiet air of efficiency. Only the occupants would be different.

The windows along the corridor were all tinted to subdue the glare and the heat of the sun's rays, and with a slight feeling of panic she hurried towards the lifts, but stopped suddenly by the one window which had clear glass and from where she could see below her the sprawling city which was Sydney. From this height the cars looked like toys, the people like ants and there were rooftops and chimneys stretching away into the hazy distance. The harbour bridge looked very much like the coathanger to which it was often compared and the ship which was passing beneath it reminded her, with a feeling of nostalgia, of the one she used to sail on the creek at home with her brother. From this height and distance it also looked like a toy.

'Terrific view, isn't it?' asked a voice behind her, and the girl spun round to face a rotund-looking man wearing a brown boiler suit. He gave her a friendly smile and glanced down at the city so far below. 'I never get tired of looking at it. You work here, miss?'

'I could have done.' As he was a stranger it did not matter what she said to him, for she would never see him again. 'But I refused the job. Because of this' —she waved her hand towards the long silent corridor—'and that.' She half turned to glance down through the window. 'I couldn't stay up here.'

'Don't you like heights?' he asked sympathetically. 'Once you're inside one of those posh offices, miss, you'd forget you were eighteen floors up.'

'Maybe.' It was not only the thought of the seventeen floors below her, it had been also the look in the eyes of the man who had interviewed her. And the thought, too, that if she screamed no one would ever hear her. Everything was muted, air-conditioned and too impersonal and isolated.

The lift doors opened silently and she turned, gave a friendly smile at the janitor and just managed to slide into the lift as the doors started to move silently together.

'I'm sorry,' said the only occupant, a girl holding an armful of manilla folders and with one of her fingers still on the button marked 'Ground'. 'I didn't realise you were coming. You've got to be quick.'

Everything, even lifts, moved at the same hurried pace, thought Irene wearily as she stepped out on the ground floor and heard the rush of traffic and the hurrying feet on the hot pavement. Her nose twitched at the smell of petrol fumes and the diesel

6

oil from the buses as they pulled away from the pavement edge, loaded to the doors, and started a grind uphill.

Half an hour later she closed the door of the flat she shared with her sister and leaned back against it, rubbing her forehead with one hand. It was dark and cool in the narrow hallway and the four small rooms which opened from it, for the venetian blinds were down, shutting out the brilliant sunshine. From the room at the end of the hall came the aroma of roast chicken and the burble of the electric jug —sounds of peace and home, she thought thankfully.

'I just timed it right, didn't I?' asked a cheerful voice. 'I knew you'd feel like a drink as soon as you came in. Unless you'd prefer something cold?'

Irene smiled at her tall fair-haired sister as she walked into the kitchen. 'No, Fran. A cup of tea is what I'm needing desperately.'

Fran looked at her keenly and her heart sank as she noticed the tired eyes and the droop of the slender shoulders.

'No luck?' she asked quietly.

'Oh, yes, there was one job there for the taking. But I received the impression that in taking it I'd also be taking on the boss as well! He had that kind of look in his eyes.' There was an understanding chuckle from her sister. 'But even if I'd liked him I couldn't have worked in that office. It was on the eighteenth floor——' She shivered and a warm hand rested lightly on her head for a moment as Fran

7

passed behind her with the teapot held firmly in the other hand. 'There was another I could have had too, but that was in one of those back streets near Central Station, and all that could be seen through the windows were hoardings, garbage bins at the back of some small factory and the men's!'

A cup of tea was handed across the table and Fran sat down to face her as Irene went on, 'All those buildings are so impersonal, they go straight up and down and have no personalities, they're so strictly utilitarian. I was spoilt, I suppose,' she said reflectively. 'And I do wish my dear old Mr Finlayson hadn't died. He was always so courteous and kind and I felt secure in that old-fashioned, comfortable office in the cool stone building, with my window looking out on to a jacaranda tree. Fran, it always looked so different, did that tree. In late winter it was bare and I could see the clouds, then it flowered and the whole of the window space was filled with the bracts of those huge bluey-mauve bells. Then later, in the summer, the fernlike leaves touched the window pane——' She lifted her cup to her lips to hide their trembling, knowing as she did so that it was impossible to hide her distress from the keen eyes of Fran, who apart from being her only relative in the city was also a nursing Sister in one of Sydney's largest hospitals. So little escaped that placid gaze.

'And so?' Fran had her elbows on the table with her cup held between her hands.

'I'll have to look through more columns of the

8

papers, I suppose.' The sigh which accompanied those words made Fran wince. The voice sounded so hopeless and defeated.

The elder by five years, Fran loved her sister deeply, and upon the death of their father she had implored her to leave the country and come and live with her in the flat not so far from the waters of Sydney harbour. Now she knew she had made a big mistake in persuading Irene to come south; city life obviously did not suit her and the traffic and the always hurrying populace upset her. Though she had not remarked upon it she was amazed and frightened of the way, since the sudden death of the old solicitor who had been more of a father figure than an employer, Irene's face had lost its colour and her whole attitude seemed to have altered. She was no longer the exuberant tomboy they had all known, all her elfin charm seemed to have withered away. She watched as her sister reached for the paper.

'Let me look,' she suggested, and without hesitation the thick folds were handed over. 'There seems to be plenty to choose from,' she remarked, glancing down the list of Positions Vacant, 'but they don't always say whereabouts they are. Oh, listen to this! "Fabulous city company desires jazzy secretary for office in the centre of the city. Gorgeous atmosphere in very mod office with an employer who will make your life blissful." '

'That sounds like the man I met this afternoon,' commented Irene with a grimace.

'Here's another. "Secretary wanted for the world

of advertising. If you have initiative, competence and are well groomed and well mannered, this is definitely the job for you." ' A tiny smile crossed Irene's face as she reached for the teapot and feeling somewhat heartened, Fran went on, her eyes glancing swiftly down the many long columns, ' "Secretary. An excellent position for the girl who likes to run the show. Company director desires one to be his right hand." ' At that they both laughed. 'Such adverts would put off all the nice girls,' said Fran. 'There are plenty in accountancy, engineering and stockbrokers' offices, as well as legal——'

'Somehow I don't feel like going back to typing out wills, codicils, house transfers and divorce proceedings. I'd like something different.'

'Yet you have all the legal terms and technicalities at your fingertips.'

'I know.' Irene hesitated. 'Try the situations vacant columns,' she said casually.

'Housekeepers? Cooks? Oh, you infant, there'd be nothing suitable for you!' Fran looked surprised at the way her sister glanced at her. 'Surely you aren't serious? You couldn't cope as a mother's help or a governess.'

'I would try if it would mean not having to spend the daylight hours sitting on top of a skyscraper!' There sounded to be a definite little snap in the words and Fran bent her head again.

'Barmaid. Counterhand. Housemaid. Oh!' There was silence as Fran read the advertisement which had caught her eyes for the second time. 'Just listen to this,' she said slowly. 'Companion required for elderly lady residing in Northern Tasmania. Duties include secretarial work and good speeds and accurate typing are essential. Must be capable driver with unblemished record, be fond of animals and like quiet surroundings as the position offered is five miles from the nearest town. Good salary to the right person!" Whoever it is sounds to want a lot for the money, so the salary would need to be good!' She lifted her head. 'Why, Irene!'

'Is there an address?'

'A box number. Surely you aren't——'

'My shorthand and typing are as good as anyone else's. I have a clean driving record—how could it be anything else when I haven't driven a car since coming down here? Not in Sydney's traffic—I'm a bush wallah! I like cats and dogs, and at the moment I certainly want quiet surroundings.' Irene looked at her sister defiantly as though Fran was going to dispute all those things. Then her expression changed. 'You said Tasmania?'

'What's that got to do with it?'

There was a long silence. Irene picked up a teaspoon and stirred the few tea-leaves in the bottom of her cup. 'If I was lucky enough to get the job what would you do?' she asked at last. 'About the flat? Would it mean giving it up?'

'What would I do?' Fran cried quickly. 'Get married! Then Bill could come and live here with me until he's completed this course and gained his degree. He needs someone to look after him, he can't concentrate on his studies when he has to cook and clean the shop and look after himself in that poky hole he calls home at the Cross! But you aren't serious in answering this?'

'I am.'

The advertisement was read again. 'It sounds all right,' Fran admitted grudgingly. 'But I wonder why they advertise in the Sydney papers; there must be hundreds of girls in Tasmania who are quite capable of filling the position. Perhaps the five miles from the nearest town is the snag. Not that it would worry you.'

'Not after living thirty-five from one in the country. I could walk those five miles into town and enjoy it. Where's the writing paper?'

Fran thought suddenly that there was more animation in the delicately moulded face of the younger girl than she had seen for a long time. She watched Irene lift her portable typewriter on to the table and studied the slim figure with affection. Five foot two, slightly built, the pale face crowned by a mass of nut-brown hair and beneath the forehead a pair of brown eyes which, for some reason, often reminded her of the cocker spaniel she had owned for years when they lived in the old house. Trustful eyes, too trustful for their owner to be at large in a huge city. Though she would certainly miss her sister if she left, either to go to Tasmania or to return to the town nearest to where they had lived, Bill would take her place and if Irene would be happier living away she would not raise any objections. Besides, the child was old enough to know what she wanted.

As she watched the slim busy fingers she hoped this elderly lady who wanted a typist-cum-driver-cum-kennelmaid would find something in the letter which would appeal to her, sufficient to make her want to meet the writer.

'There!' Somewhat triumphantly Irene withdrew the paper, read the letter carefully again and signed her name. 'Does that sound all right to you?'

Fran hid a smile as she read it. All Irene's capabilities were explained with a precision which brought back memories of the old solicitor; it was businesslike but there was a touch of youth in the simple sentence at the end. 'I hope to hear from you soon.'

'I put the phone number at the top too. Maybe if there are no more applicants they'll ring me.'

Fran stood up, thinking it was doubtful if anyone would phone from Tasmania. 'That explains everything very neatly. You're going to post it now? I'll get changed, because Bill is free tonight and we thought we'd have a night out on the tiles for a change.'

Irene laughed at the thought of her sister and her quiet studious fiancé painting the town red. They would, in all probability, spend their evening discussing various cases at the hospital and making plans for their future together. Fran would make a wonderful wife for a doctor.

During the next few days Irene made a pretence

of going into the city as she had no wish for Fran to realise how desperately she was hoping for an affirmative reply to her letter. She had three interviews at different offices and turned down flat the offer of the second; the third she was not given the chance to do so, for the prospective employer announced, almost before she had opened the door to confront him, that the position was filled. He wondered at the warmth óf the smile which greeted this news.

By the end of the week the hope which had so buoyed her after posting the letter gradually died away and Fran watched her with concern. She made no comment, for what was there to say? Irene's application would certainly not be the only one; replies would come from others equally proficient. She noticed that the morning paper was always opened at the same page and flung down, as though in disgust, and wished her sister would decide to return to the country and be happy, maybe even finding another job in an office where there was a tree outside the window and a benign-bespectacled old dear such as Mr Finlayson sitting, stiff-backed, on the other side of a wide desk.

All hope fled from Irene's mind on the eighth day after posting the letter. By now someone else would be driving the five miles into town with the old lady sitting beside her nursing a couple of poodles, or sitting in front of a fire taking down dictation as cold winds blew in from the sea.

Fran was on night duty for two weeks and so, when the telephone did ring loudly early one morning,

Irene made a grab at it before the shrill 'brr-brr' awakened her sister and brought a sleepy call to ask if it was for her.

'Miss Peterson?' It was a nice brisk voice and immediately Irene thought of one of the doctors, or even one of the specialists.

'Do you want Sister Peterson?'

'Miss Irene Peterson.'

'Oh, that's me!' she exclaimed in relief. Fran had looked so very tired when she had come in just turned eight o'clock and in reply to a quietly asked question had said briefly, 'Yes, a very bad night.'

'My name is Morgan. You answered an advertisement for a companion-secretary for a position in Tasmania.'

Irene felt stunned. She closed her eyes and leaned against the wall, clutching the phone as though it was her last link with the world and she dared not let it slip from her fingers.

'Are you there?' asked the voice impatiently.

'Yes, oh, yes! You were saying, Mr Morgan?' Whatever would he think? That she was not capable of even answering a telephone. 'I'm sorry. Are you ringing from Tasmania?'

'Am I—no, I'm not. I'm in Sydney. I came on business with the intention of interviewing in person the three applicants for the position.'

'Of course. Yes, I see.' She hoped he would not hear the wild beating of her heart.

'Could you please make it convenient to come for an interview at three-thirty this afternoon to a motel

15

in Rose Bay?' She very breathlessly said yes and he went on to explain exactly where it was, and Irene, swallowing hard because her throat felt so dry, nodded in agreement as she listened.

'I know where it is, Mr Morgan.'

'Thank you. Until three-thirty, then. Goodbye.' The call had been brief and very businesslike and the district receiver was replaced.

Slowly Irene pivoted on her heels and stared down the hall. A personal interview. Why had she not thought of such a thing? Naturally no one was going to employ a secretary without looking her over first. Imagine going all the way to Tasmania and then being informed that she was totally unsuitable! What had the man said? Two other applicants. And those she could not dismiss from her mind with the airy thought that they would be unsuitable.

'Pull yourself together,' she told her inner self fiercely. 'Until you're informed that Mr Morgan doesn't like you or thinks you unsuitable there is hope. Now what shall I wear?'

Going into her small bedroom, she shut the door, thankful that the ringing of the phone had not awakened Fran. She opened the wardrobe door and surveyed the many suits and dresses hanging there. Mr Finlayson had been a generous employer; apart from her salary she had received bonuses at Christmas and on her birthday, and like most girls of her age she had bought all she needed and a lot she didn't. Fran liked the green two-piece; even Bill had remarked upon it, he said the colour brought out the lights in her hair, and if he thought it chic surely another man would do the same. Yes, the green linen with the little feathery hat of the same colour. She felt well groomed and comfortable in that suit, and if she was not happy with her appearance she knew she would wriggle and fidget and Mr Morgan would wonder what was the matter with her.

So much depended upon this interview, her own future and her sister's. Fran and Bill would not want to marry and share this small flat with a younger sister, and Irene quite agreed that Bill needed looking after. Hours of study, meals at odd times and varying rosters at the hospital were beginning to show their mark. With Fran to cook for him, to help him with his studies and the preparations for the all-important exams later in the year, and to love him, Bill would become a different person.

All this she explained seriously to Fran before she left the house. Sitting on the edge of her sister's bed, she told her about the phone call, and Fran, leaning on one elbow, watched the varying expressions on the youthful face with affection. She hoped desperately that Mr Morgan would not think Irene was too young; if he did the disappointment would be hard for the girl to bear.

'If you're fortunate enough to get the job,' she said quietly, 'it will mean you and I won't be able to see each other very often.'

Irene smiled. 'If I returned to the country the same thing would apply. And later when Bill gets a practice all his own you'll be tied down too, especially at the beginning.'

Fran admitted the truth of that. 'You'd better go, dear, you mustn't be late. Will you get a cab?'

Irene nodded as she kissed Fran lightly on the brow. 'I've left everything ready for you when you decide to get up. You're on duty at the same time tonight?'

'Yes, so I'll be here to listen to all you have to tell me. The very best of luck!'

It was not always easy to get a cab. Irene waited at the rank and glanced down at her watch with increasing impatience, heedless for once of the hurrying throng behind her and intent only on the passing traffic. One cab finally pulled into the kerb and a woman and a child alighted, and almost before their feet were on the ground Irene was scrambling into the rear seat. The driver turned his head as she sat down.

'I'm booked,' he stated flatly.

'And I'm in a great hurry to get to Rose Bay,' she retorted. 'The driver of every cab which has pulled in here during the last ten minutes has told me the same thing. I don't believe you!' She stopped, wondering at her audacity, for usually cab-drivers and their like had only to say 'Sorry' and shake their heads and she would step back on to the pavement and wait patiently for the next.

The driver slammed the door and moved into the stream of traffic, and he kept up a tuneless whistle the whole of the way.

'Thank you.' As she alighted she looked at him and there was something in her expression which made him smile at her; she did look rather small and sweet and defenceless, he thought reflectively.

The large glass doors swung behind her as she crossed the thickly carpeted floor and went up to the reception desk. As she asked for Mr Morgan she hoped the man behind the wide counter would not notice the tremor in her voice. He nodded and pointed with his pen towards a chair.

'Mr Morgan is engaged at the moment, so if you don't mind waiting over there——'

Irene was thankful to sink back into the deep modern chair, for her legs, for some strange reason, had the feeling of not belonging to her body.

Feeling extremely nervous about the coming interview, she concentrated her attention on the foyer, which was luxurious. It was thickly carpeted and had numerous exotic plants in large wooden tubs near the door; one side of the room was a huge picture window and through it could be seen Sydney harbour in all its glory in the afternoon sunshine. It was an intimate view, she thought happily as she watched a grey destroyer pass one of the Manly ferries. Even the gull sitting on top of the mast of a moored yacht could be seen preening its feathers, something you would never be able to see from the eighteenth floor of one of the down-town office blocks. The destroyer vanished from sight on its way to Garden Island and she turned her attention to the furnishings. One would need plenty of money to stay here, so Mr Morgan could not be in straitened circumstances. She became lost in a dream as she tried to visualise where he lived. There would be a large well-tended garden with many varieties of trees under which, when the weather was kind, the elderly lady would sit with her poodles——

'Miss Peterson!' cried a voice impatiently.

'Oh! I'm sorry.' Irene jumped to her feet and her face flushed as she looked up at the man beside her. He was tall, but most men did appear to tower above her because of her own lack of height. 'I didn't hear you, I'm afraid my thoughts were miles away,' she confessed in a low voice.

'Where?' he asked abruptly.

'I——I was thinking about trees,' she said, and changed the subject quickly. 'You're Mr Morgan?'

'I am.'

'I'm very pleased to meet you.'

'Oh!' He turned away to hide the sudden smile which crossed his face. 'Come this way, please.'

CHAPTER 2

LEADING the way into a small conference room not far from the reception desk, he indicated a chair, and obediently Irene sat down. There was a wide polished table, obviously to be used as a desk, and he sat behind it, surveying her for a moment in silence, and she met his eyes candidly. She did not fidget, her ungloved hands lay one on top of the other and her back was straight, in fact she was unconsciously doing as old Mr Finlayson had always told her to do during any interview. 'Relax, my dear. Completely relax. Let the other person start to talk. Never interrupt, just listen and answer questions briefly, truthfully and clearly.'

The man facing her had a lean rugged face with a strong mouth and chin; Irene had the impression that he could be ruthless. His hands were well kept and his suit, she noticed critically, was tailored in a very fine worsted tweed and the colour of his tie was subdued. How different from some of the men with whom she had had interviews, and she thought briefly of one who had been sitting, or lolling would be the better word, behind an untidy cluttered desk, with his coat discarded, his shirt sleeves rolled up and with the knot of his tie resting down on his chestbone.

Mr Morgan moved some papers, cleared his throat

and asked quietly, 'Why did you answer the advertisement, Miss Peterson?'

'Because my former employer died suddenly a few weeks ago and I want another position,' she answered without hesitation.

'So you have no references?'

She stared at him. This was the first time anyone had mentioned such things. 'No, I'm sorry. It was the only job I had in Sydney.'

'Why do you want to go to Tasmania?'

'I don't like cities,' was the blunt answer, and he smiled slightly. The smile softened the ruggedness of his jaw and mentally she readjusted the feeling of him being ruthless. 'And I've heard much about the island—I believe it's very beautiful.'

'It is,' he agreed. 'I see by your letter that you're a neat typist. Your shorthand speed?' There was another brief answer and he nodded. 'Who was your former employer?'

'Mr William Finlayson, a solicitor. I was with him for over four years and I could get references from his many friends and business associates.'

He nodded again and made a note on a paper in front of him. 'And your driving ability?'

'I drove all over my father's property even when I was at school and got my licence when I was seventeen. There are no black marks against it.' A tiny dimple appeared on one cheek as she said the words with pride.

'So you're a country girl?'

'Yes. My mother died when I was young and when

Dad died a few years ago my brother and his wife took over the management of the property. I came down here to live with my sister—she's a double certificated nurse.' That was the whole history of the Peterson family in a nutshell.

'And to live five miles from town wouldn't worry you?' There was a definite shake of her head. 'And you would be used to animals?' This time there was a brief 'Yes' in reply. 'You aren't very talkative,' he observed, leaning back in the chair, his keen eyes looking straight into hers.

'You're interviewing me, Mr Morgan,' she replied quietly, and to her amazement he laughed.

The girl who had preceded her had talked all through the very brief interview, and as he was the prospective employer he felt it was his right to ask the questions. He had informed her, as he stood up to signify that he was terminating the conversation and also the interview, that he was sorry but she would not be at all suitable for the position, and had received a toss of the head in reply. She had swiftly made up her mind about working for this man and the others he had mentioned. The girl who should have been at the motel at two-thirty had not arrived, neither had she bothered to phone him.

'How old are you, Miss Peterson?'

'Twenty-one.'

'And do you think you would have the patience to spend a great deal of your time, most of it in fact, in the company of someone who's crippled?'

For the first time Irene hesitated. 'I could only

23

promise to do my best. I have little knowledge of nursing——'

'That wouldn't be necessary. My aunt, on whose behalf I'm interviewing you, had an accident a few years ago and uses a wheelchair. But she's by no means an invalid—with help she can get into a car and into bed, and her housekeeper, who's been with her for a very long time, is most helpful in that respect. My cousin and I also assist whenever we can. That's one reason why I'm insistent that a good driving record is essential, for she must have confidence in the person who drives her round the countryside and to visit her friends. It's she who requires a secretary, as she's a prolific writer of articles on many varied subjects and also of short stories.' He studied Irene, taking in every detail of the green suit, the brown hair peeping out from beneath the green feathers of the cute little hat, the steady brown eyes and the slightly trembling mouth. The girl was nervous but was trying desperately not to let him see it. He put his elbows on the desk and clasped his hands beneath his chin and the ruthlessness appeared to vanish altogether as he half smiled.

'You were thinking about trees when I introduced myself,' he murmured. 'Do you like them?'

'Oh, yes!' Irene leaned forward confidingly and her lips curved into a smile. 'They're some of the things I miss so much down here. Our house in the country was surrounded by trees of all descriptions, some planted by my grandparents, and those were tall and shady and threw shadows over the lawns on the hot days. The rest were put in by my mother, who must have had green fingers——' She stopped. Mr Finlayson would have strongly disapproved of that burst of confidence.

'And if necessary you could feed a poddy lamb and wouldn't be scared of bullocks?'

'Bullocks?' Irene's eyes opened wide. 'I'd thought of poodles!'

Carl Morgan laughed with unconcealed enjoyment. How naïve she was! And how different was her face when the seriousness vanished. 'Why poodles?' he enquired.

'It was just—from the advertisement—I was sure there would be dogs.'

'There are dogs. All kinds of animals because my cousin is a vet. He has boarding kennels with a small hospital and even a little operating theatre where on rare occasions I've been the anaesthetist. We get various lame, weak, ill-treated and unwanted animals to look after; he brings them into the house to be fussed over and nursed and we're expected to show as much enthusiasm about their recovery as he does. Does the thought alarm you?'

'Not at all,' she cried, remembering the lambs she had forcibly fed, the puppies she had fussed over, the young off the farm who had been brought into the home paddocks for attention. 'It sounds like fun!' she corrected herself hastily. 'Like old times.'

'So you'll be willing to go to Tasmania?'

'You—you mean I have the job?' The brown eyes widened with disbelief.

'Yes, you have.' His smile broadened and her heart gave a queer little jump. 'If you'll accept it.'

'Yes, gladly!'

'Without even knowing the wage I intend offering you?'

She flushed again. Money had become a secondary consideration. The very thought of living in the country with this man's aunt and cousin, among trees and animals, in an atmosphere more like the one in which she had been brought up, had filled her with thankfulness. The amount he offered was most satisfactory and she was smiling as she stood up.

'Tell me, please,' she said shyly, her face upturned to his. 'Why did you advertise in the Sydney papers for a secretary for your aunt?'

'Because the girls we've had recently live too near home. They had relatives who were always sick, going away or getting married, they had boy-friends who always wanted them to finish at a certain hour, and if my aunt really gets into her stride she hates to be disturbed or broken off. In fact she became infuriated and sacked more than one girl because she refused to stay that little extra time. So to have someone to live in, to be on call whenever inspiration came to her, Aunt Kate decided to have someone from far away. I'm warning you now, Miss Peterson, that you may find yourself taking dictation with your breakfast or your supper, on Saturdays, Sundays and public holidays, in the car or on a beach, even on a headland in a howling gale. Anything is likely to stir her imagination. She's also a great conservationist and has forceful ideas on that subject.' A gleam came into his eyes as he said that. 'But it won't be all work and no play. Aunt is a very generous woman, if she thinks she's worked you too hard one week she may send you away for a few days —then you'll get a telegram asking you to return as she wants all her alterations, additions and erasures of her latest brain-child typed again immediately. Do you still want to go?'

'Yes,' she said emphatically.

'I have your phone number and will ring you tomorrow evening, if that's convenient, to give you the time and date of your departure from Sydney. My cousin will meet the plane at Devonport and drive you home.'

Irene turned to smile at him again as she reached the door; her eyes were dancing and her whole expression could only be described, he thought, as one of mischievous delight. Very thoughtfully he stared at the graining of the wood on the door after she had closed it quietly behind her, then he turned to the desk, pulled the phone towards him and dialled a number. When a voice answered he said,

'Carl. Yes, Mac—do you remember a William Finlayson who died a few weeks ago? He was a solicitor—yes. What kind of a man was he? One of the old school—yes, I know, there aren't many of them left these days. You would also know his secretary?' The voice at the other end of the line spoke rapidly and Carl nodded as he listened. 'I thought so too. She's just been in here applying for the position of secretary-companion to Aunt Kate. She looks very small and defenceless and I'm quite sure Alex will be the first to rush and take her into his care! Her qualifications should also please my aunt. Why, thanks, I'd love a game of golf——'

Irene travelled home in a daze of happiness. No more searching the papers for a suitable position, no more travelling in crowded trains or buses, no more interviews——

'No more men leering at me across a desk, no more tall buildings,' she cried as she flung the feathered hat on top of the kitchen cabinet with a flourish. There was a sparkle in her eye and a flush on her cheeks. 'Oh, Fran I've got the job!' Words could not come out quickly enough as she described all that had been said.

'A writer and a vet!' Fran started to laugh. 'Oh, my dear, you're sure to have plenty of variety in your life from now on! The aunt sounds to be a delightful person, as does her son. Where does Mr Morgan come into all this?'

'I don't know, I didn't ask him.' The dimple appeared as Irene chuckled. 'But he must live with them, for he referred to the place as home. The salary is excellent, don't you think so?'

'It all sounds to be exactly as you wanted it to be. But you won't be able to escape so easily.'

'I don't think I'll want to,' murmured Irene, lowering her eyes, and her sister looked at her very thoughtfully as she wondered what this Mr Morgan was really like.

'You know, don't you, dear, that if things don't fall into place as you so obviously think they will, you can always return to us here.'

Bill said exactly the same thing when he escorted Irene to the airport four days later. It was his day off, and as Fran was on duty their farewells had been said early in the morning before she left for the hospital.

'If you don't like either the place or the people,' he said seriously and firmly, 'you mustn't hesitate to come back. There's always a home waiting for you with Frances and myself.'

'I know that, and thank you.' Irene looked into his thin clever face. He was so tired; the best thing that could happen to him was marriage to Fran. Strange how he always insisted on calling her Frances; she had never heard him refer to her sister or call her any other name. Except darling. 'It will be pleasant to always have that thought at the back of my mind,' she added, knowing that the last thing she would do once they were married would be to become a third in the small flat.

She clung to him when the moment of departure arrived. 'Look after Fran,' she whispered huskily. 'And do take care of yourself. I wish I could be here for your wedding, but I couldn't ask Mr Morgan to wait another month.'

'We quite understand. This is the chance you've been waiting for. Good luck!' He kissed her and gave her hand a comforting squeeze, then watched as she hurried across the tarmac to where the big jet was standing. Irene did not look back.

The flight to Melbourne was swift and uneventful. There she had a short wait and then boarded the second plane for the flight across Bass Strait, which was made within the hour. Her pulses quickened as they neared the coast and she saw Tasmania for the first time, as the plane banked a little a river showed like a blue streak between the green and a man sitting beside her informed her that it was the River Mersey. One more circle and they landed smoothly. Clutching her handbag and a small travelling case, she went down the steps and walked towards the terminal buildings, wondering how she would recognise Alex Marron. When he had phoned her that the tickets would be waiting for her to pick up at the airline office Irene had felt a surge of annoyance at the casual tone of Mr Morgan's voice as he assured her that his cousin would be there to meet her, adding that he would have no difficulty in picking her out from the other passengers. She had been left to wonder just what he meant—surely she was not so conspicuous?

Most of the other passengers were holidaymakers, although a few were greeted by relatives. They waited in small talkative groups for the luggage to be unloaded, then cars and taxis were driven away and gradually a silence settled on the airport. Irene looked round with apprehension in her eyes. A couple of men were moving away from one of the buildings and neither glanced in her direction, one of the officials almost ran from the office to his car and shot away down the road as though he was taking off after the plane which was by now a speck in the sky on its return journey to the mainland. There was no one here to claim her and although she had the address of the place where she was to go there were no taxis and all she could do was wait. If she wandered off on her own and he arrived shortly afterwards there would be a mix-up at the very beginning of their acquaintance, and she had no desire to start off with any misunderstandings.

The sun was pleasantly warm on her face and the land stretching towards the sea looked green and inviting, but at this moment the girl was in no mood to appreciate the beauty and softness of it all. She kept glancing at her watch, walking first one way and then the other, turning to stare anxiously at the busy road in the distance and wishing one of the numerous cars would make the turn into the airport and come to a stop beside her.

Twenty minutes later her wish was granted. She watched the green station waggon come down the road; it was being driven very slowly and carefully and she wondered wildly, if this was Alex Marron at last, if he was an old man and his mother at least twenty years his senior. She realised how few questions she had asked about the people she was to meet and bit her lip as the waggon came towards her and glided gently to a stop.

The man who stepped from it was not old. He was tousle-haired and had rather a grubby look about him and bits of straw hanging from his shirt; as he came swiftly towards her she could see streaks of dirt on his cheeks.

'It can only be Miss Peterson, waiting alone and looking so lost and forlorn.' He stopped in front of her. 'I'm most awfully sorry to be so late, but it wasn't really my fault, I left home in plenty of time and I do hope you weren't thinking I wasn't going to arrive. You must have thought some dreadful things about me.' He thrust out his hand and gave hers a hearty shake. 'Carl mentioned me—I'm Alex, his cousin, and Cinderella was the reason for the delay, she's in the car now. Is this your luggage? I hope we can get it all in front. I don't think we should disturb her any more than we can help at the moment.'

Wide-eyed, Irene stared at him. He was not much older than she was and below the tousled hair were a pair of laughing blue eyes, while above his lips were more dirty streaks, as though he had wiped his hands roughly across his mouth.

'I suppose I do look a bit of a ruffian at the moment,' he said ruefully, aware of her scrutiny. 'But believe me, I'm quite respectable when I'm cleaned up! It was all her fault——' he waved towards the car. 'Oh, welcome to Tasmania! Mum said I must be sure to welcome you as Carl told us you hadn't been here before. She's looking forward to having you at Glendene.' He bent and picked up her two suitcases and clutching the bag and the travelling case Irene moved after him. 'You haven't said anything. Are you very mad at me for being so late?' he asked as he glanced over his shoulder.

'Not at all.' Her lips twitched. 'I haven't had much chance to say anything, have I?'

His face creased into smiles. 'Of course you haven't. So far I've done all the talking, but when you get used to me you'll have plenty to say for yourself and no doubt will butt in rudely upon my conversations. And if you say now what I think you will I promise not to be offended, because this'—he stopped beside the station waggon—'is Cinderella, and I'm afraid you'll have to put up with her until we get home.'

Irene stared through the window. 'Cinderella?' she said faintly.

'I called her that because she's just had a bit of a ball.'

'Oh!' She put her hands to her lips, raised her eyes and as she met his twinkling ones she went off into a peal of delighted laughter, and Cinderella, lying at ease on the straw and sacking in the back, raised her head from the contemplation of her ten piglets and grunted gently in disapproval.

With the laughter any doubts that lay at the back of her mind about the position she had taken so far away from everyone and everything she knew vanished for ever. She felt completely at ease with this young man and when she regained her breath she pressed her face close to the window and murmured, 'Aren't they cute!'

'They weren't supposed to arrive until long after I got home,' he explained as he pushed the suitcases into the front. 'I'd promised her owner to pick her

33

up, as he had been taken ill, and as even pigs have pedigrees he was worried he couldn't look after her. Whether it was the excitement of the chase to catch her or the ride I don't know, but we had to stop on the other side of Devonport. I heard the plane come in and leave again and felt dreadful at the thought of you waiting all on your lonesome, but I just couldn't rush things.'

'Of course not. I quite understand.'

'Carl told us you'd lived on a property, so I hoped you would. 'He pushed his hair back impatiently and left another dirty streak. 'If you're ready, Miss Peterson?'

'Irene,' she said as she turned from the window.

'It would have come to that within the next few minutes,' he smiled down at her.

As they drove through Devonport he described the history of the town and from what she saw of it she hoped to visit it often. He slowed through Ulverstone to let her see the unique Shrine of Remembrance and seven miles further on he turned away from the sea and drove towards a low rugged range of hills on the skyline. It was very beautiful country, dotted here and there with small farms surrounded by lush pastures, and by turning her head and looking over the recumbent form behind her she could still see the sea.

'The five miles from town won't worry you?' asked Alex.

She shook her head and described the wide open plains of New South Wales where she had been born and spent the greater part of her life, where five miles was often the distance from a house to the nearest main road.

'That sounds woeful!' he exclaimed. 'You'll like this much better. I was born at Glendene, it's been in our family for over a hundred years.' He glanced down at her. 'Carl told you Mum is crippled?'

Irene nodded. 'Was it a car accident?'

'No. She was thrown from a horse, then it fell on her and injured her lower spine.' His jaw looked stiff and she changed the subject.

'Does Carl—Mr Morgan live with you?'

'At the moment. His mother and mine are sisters and as Aunt Helen is overseas Carl moved in with us. No sense in keeping that big house open for one bloke on his own. It's another place with quite a history. Now we turn off here and soon we'll be home.'

She leaned forward in her seat and gazed ahead, along the gravelly road towards a thicket of trees which blotted out the sight of anything behind them. Somewhere there must be an opening—then Alex turned the wheel and she saw a gate nearly hidden by thick foliage; it was open and once beyond it a white road, wide enough for only one car, wriggled its way through more trees, higher and more elegant-looking than those which formed the border of the property, towards an old Colonial house with wide verandahs and with—she caught her breath in disbelief—a shingle roof. There were many chimneys, silent evidence of the severity of the Tasmanian winter, and from one a faint curl of smoke drifted into the still air. There were wide flower beds glowing with the colour of dahlias of every variety on either side of the steps leading to the white-painted front door, and she was swift to notice that a ramp had been made alongside, evidently to enable Mrs Marron to move from the house to the garden with comparative ease.

'Glendene,' said Alex softly and proudly. 'Do you feel it welcomes you?'

'Yes,' she murmured, looking at it, safe and serene in the late afternoon sunshine. 'It certainly does.'

CHAPTER 3

'IF you don't mind, we won't stop here,' said Alex. 'I think it will be better if we unload at the tradesman's instead of the guests' entrance. Netta would certainly have a lot to say if we trailed through the house with eleven swine!'

Irene chuckled. 'Netta?'

'Our housekeeper, cook and everything else you can think of. She does everything and has everything, including a broad bosom I used to cry on years ago.' She had a sudden mental picture of this young man weeping on the housekeeper's bosom and after glancing at her face Alex murmured, 'You get the picture? Even Carl did it on rare occasions!'

Surely Carl Morgan was too masculine to ever do such a thing, she thought wildly, remembering again the tall figure standing by the desk in the motel. The car swerved and they drove towards a number of outbuildings with pens and kennels and from them rose a chorus of welcoming barks, yaps, squeals and grunts as the station waggon came into sight.

'The boarding house,' was the explanation. 'There's the hospital over there—I do hope Carl explained what I do to earn an honest cent?'

'Yes, but I didn't expect such a neat set-up.'

'I have also a small surgery in town and that keeps

37

me busy too. There's never a dull moment when I'm around!'

'I believe you!' she said, smiling, and asked, as they came to a stop, 'Is there anything I can do to help?'

'If you wouldn't mind shifting some of the babies while I try and remove their mother I'd be grateful.'

There was much grunting as Cinderella was moved and with three of the small wriggling babies in her arms Irene moved towards the pen indicated. On her way back for the second trio she heard the sound of wheels on gravel and turned her head. Coming towards her was a woman in a wheelchair; her lips were compressed and she looked angry.

'Alexander!'

Alex lifted his head and his face coloured slightly as he met his mother's eyes. The chair came to an abrupt stop and the girl stood where she was holding one piglet in her arms, but she was ignored for the moment.

'I expected you back well over an hour ago! What on earth have you been doing? And did I not talk to you about this? On no account, I said, were you to drag Miss Peterson into your work out here unless it was absolutely necessary. We've all been dragged into it on occasions, and though none of us mind helping out when you're very busy it's not right that a newcomer should be so imposed upon. She's only just arrived and is already messing about with pigs!'

The chair was swivelled round and Irene was face to face with her employer. Before her accident Mrs

Marron must have been a tall woman and she had a proud lift to her snow-white head, but she looked painfully thin. Irene had yet to discover the strength of her shoulders and arms. A light rug covered her knees and as she waited the girl saw a slight softening of the eyes which were as blue as her son's. She watched the smile curve the elder woman's lips and with her left hand took hold of the one extended to her.

'So you're Irene.' The shrewd eyes looked her up and down, taking in every detail of her face and appearance. Small like one of the puppies, she thought. Shy? Or uncertain? The girl looked fragile and she wondered for a fleeting moment if she would be capable of hard work. But Carl had been emphatic that this was the type of person his aunt needed, and as Carl was rarely wrong in these matters, although he was very wrong and very stubborn in others, she was ready to accept his assurance.

'Definitely you're as Carl described you to me,' she murmured. 'Welcome to Glendene, and accept my apologies for the way my son has traded upon your good nature within minutes of your arrival. Look at your lovely coat! Really, Alex, this is too much!'

'I don't mind—honestly!' protested Irene quickly. 'He couldn't look after Cinderella and the ten little ones all at once.'

'When they rang you,' Mrs Marron spun round the other way, 'it was because of one sow. There was no mention of any progeny!'

'No,' Alex smiled at her. 'They arrived just outside Devonport on my way in to the 'drome.'

For a moment she looked at him, then at Irene, at the snorting, grunting Cinderella and the newly born piglet the girl still held in her arms.

'There's no answer to that one, is there?' she asked, shaking her head. 'Put the animal with the others and then let Alex attend to the rest. After waiting all that time you must be ready for a meal and a drink. Come with me and I'll introduce you to my housekeeper; she'll look after you and attend to all your needs.'

Netta was round like a pudding with a broad plump face; she was kind and possessive to those she thought of as her own, but with Irene her manner was curt as Mrs Marron made the introductions. Never before had a girl from the mainland come to work at Glendene; always they had lived locally or within travelling distance of their homes, and it had been easy for Netta to put out of countenance those of whom she disapproved or if she thought they trespassed beyond what she thought was the limit they could go with her beloved mistress.

She was old-fashioned in many ways too and had been very outspoken on occasions about the manners and the habits of the girls who had lived in the house for any length of time. With this one she was wary, for she had come from across the sea, so there would be no returning to the maternal roof at the weekends, no requests for days or evenings off. What had Carl been thinking about to choose one as small and as fragile-looking as this girl? She would have something to say to him upon his return home.

'This is your room,' she said abruptly, flinging back a door and standing on one side as Alex brought in the suitcases, and then waved along the hallway. 'The bathroom is there, and you'll be needing a shower after handling those pigs!' It was a definite command to freshen up immediately and Irene nodded meekly in agreement.

The room was small but charming. The bed with its carved headboard must have been one of the original pieces of furniture in the house; it looked old-fashioned and sturdy, and after shutting the door Irene poked at it tentatively and then sat on it, To her relief she discovered there was a modern inner-spring mattress which promised comfort. The thick eiderdown reminded her again that she was in a cooler climate and she could imagine snuggling down beneath it on a cold night and pulling it up round her ears.

The ceiling was very low and the window was small. Irene almost gave a whoop of delight when she looked out, for there was a tree whose branches were within inches of the glass and hanging from them were apples, rosy where they had been touched with the sun. Through the leaves she could see the countryside, mellow now in the fading afternoon and out on the horizon, jutting up against the sky-line, was one solitary peak.

After a hot shower and a change of clothing she realised she was hungry and made her way uncertainly along the hall, wondering in which room Mrs Marron would be waiting for her.

'In here!' Netta called, and Irene turned into what was the kitchen, which was low-ceilinged and warm. A large table filled the centre of the room; it was covered by a yellow check cloth and the housekeeper was already lifting the teapot. A huge golden labrador lifted his head, surveyed the newcomer with querying eyes and ambled from the rug to inspect her, sniffing at her shoes and then at her outstretched hand. Evidently Irene was accepted, for he gave a wag of his tail and settled down again with a sigh of content, facing the warmth of the oven.

'Brutus,' was Netta's introduction. 'My dog.'

There was a large box on the floor; something black moved within it and the girl bent over to smile at the four tiny bodies which were pressed against each other.

'Kittens. Someone dumped them near the gate knowing full well they would be looked after.' Netta sniffed in disapproval and poured out the tea. 'I wish it was possible to dump some humans, there's a lot we could do without!' She passed over a plate of warm scones, a jug of thick cream and a dish of what was obviously home-made strawberry jam. 'Think you're going to like it here?' she asked abruptly. 'We're a long way from town.'

'Five miles! My old home was thirty-five miles from the nearest township. I've been living in Sydney, and you have no idea how I'm going to appreciate being in the country again.'

'Early days yet.' There was an ominous note in her voice which Irene chose to ignore.

'And to have a tree right outside my window——'

'And that obviously pleases you,' remarked a voice behind her, and she turned.

Alex looked so different without the dirt on his face, with his hair brushed and wearing clean clothes. He seemed to have gained in stature and become quite good-looking. Most of all it was the laughter in his eyes which appealed to her.

'Netta, how on earth do you expect the girl to keep her petite figure if you give her all that cream?' he asked as he sat down. 'She'll finish up looking like you!'

'It'll be no bad thing to have a bit more flesh on her bones. Get that pig settled?'

He nodded as he reached for the jam, then the door was flung back and his mother wheeled herself into the room, followed by another dog which had no claim at all to a pedigree. Irene guessed it was another who had been dumped near the gate.

'So this is where you are! I've been waiting for you, Irene, as I was going to talk while you had afternoon tea—there's much I want to discuss.' There was a note of censure in her voice and Irene glanced uncomfortably at the housekeeper. Netta answered casually,

'Thought she could have it in here. I'd just made a new brew.'

'In that case I'll have one too, though I would have preferred it in my study.'

'In winter this is the warmest and the most pleas-ant room in the house,' said her son, ignoring her obvious irritation. 'I used to love it when I was a kid. Even my high and mighty cousin finds his way in here.'

'Carl comes to see me,' stated Netta flatly, moving round the table, and after making sure Mrs Marron was comfortable and within easy reach of everything, she placed a cup of tea before her. 'And to sample my cooking. He appreciates good meals.'

'We all do that, beloved,' he assured her, and turned to the girl at his side. 'I'm going to show you all I've been doing during the past three years——'

'Time enough for that,' was his mother's tart reply. 'Irene has already made the acquaintance of one of your patients, the rest can wait.'

The implication being, thought Irene, that she was here as Mrs Marron's secretary and Alex and his work was out of bounds except at odd moments. She changed the subject.

'From my window I can see the tip of what looks like a mountain.' There was a question in her voice.

'St Valentine's Peak,' Mrs Marron nodded. 'We'll go out that way tomorrow and you'll see it even more clearly, though we can't get very close to it.'

Alex glanced at her across the table. The road to which she referred was tricky and had to be driven over with care. His mother would soon realise a driver's capabilities, and he looked at Irene's slim wrists and rather delicate hands and wondered if she would have the strength to drive the big car

44

round some of the bends and up the many gradients. Now his mother had become so wrapped up and interested in conservation that there would be many more drives to even more inaccessible places. He remembered one girl who had driven his mother for the first time; she had received a parking ticket and another for speeding the second time they went out. That had been the end of her stay at Glendene, and at the memory of what had been said by two angry women he smiled. The three at the table looked at him.

'Merely a passing thought,' he said airily, surveying each face in turn.

'On occasions I would dearly love to be able to see what goes on inside your head,' remarked his mother reflectively.

'It's as well you can't,' he retorted, and she laughed.

'Now, if you're ready, Irene?' the white eyebrows were raised and immediately the girl stood up, 'we'll explore the house. Oh, this is Lulu.' Irene acknowledged the introduction seriously as the nondescript little dog politely raised a paw. 'I can manage alone, thank you, the house is all on one level and provision has been made for me to get in and out of doors without troubling anyone. I haven't lost all my independence.'

She whizzed off down the main hallway, which must have been eight feet wide, to stop abruptly before a huge chest of drawers which looked beautiful and valuable.

'Huon pine, made for the first Marron who built this house so long ago. No one could make such a piece of furniture today—the skill isn't there, nor the attention given to detail.'

Off she went again, and Irene followed, her eyes missing nothing. The furniture was old and in excellent condition, polished through the years by many loving hands. The rooms were light and airy and each had a view of the countryside; it was a much larger house than it looked to be from the outside.

'Now here is where you will spend much of your time.' The door swung back at a touch and the wheelchair came to a halt.

The floor-to-ceiling windows overlooked the garden at the side of the house and caught the westerly sun. The long drapes on either side were a restful shade of green and the floor was thickly carpeted in a deeper shade. A neat little basket was on the rug in front of the now empty fireplace and Lulu stepped into it and watched them with bright eyes. The large desk with a covered typewriter in the centre was across a corner so the light would be over Irene's shoulder. A low table was covered with letters, papers and leaflets, and many well filled bookshelves were nearby. Beside the fireplace was a highly polished brass box which obviously held the logs necessary to heat the room, and she felt a thrill of pleasure at the thought of being in here on a cold winter's day, with the dancing flames to keep her company as she attended to her secretarial duties.

Mrs Marron explained that she had many friends who were always welcome, other writers who came for advice and discussion, as well as government officials and others who were interested in conservation and her literature regarding it. Irene listened intently, but when the other described some of the places she wished to visit the girl felt the first pang of doubt.

How would she fare behind the wheel of the car for the first time? It was so long since she had driven anywhere, and it was all very well informing Mr Morgan that her licence was in order and she had no black marks against it when of recent times she had not had any practice. Driving along unfamiliar roads in an unfamiliar car with someone of experience sitting behind her and watching every move was a totally different proposition from what she had been used to in the country, in an old jalopy, on roads where other traffic was almost negligible and through villages where on occasion cows wandered down the main street.

After returning from the kennels where he had said goodnight to all the inmates and comforted as best he could a large shaggy dog who was pining for the large family who used to play with him, take him out and cry into his fur when they had been chastised and wanted his silent comfort, Alex stood in the half light and looked at the large sedan which had been bought for the sole purpose of enabling his mother to sit in comfort. She always sat in the back and commented lightly that she made an excel-

lent back seat driver—a remark he knew covered
her great feeling of frustration at being dependent
on others and not being able to go where she wanted,
when she wanted. Thoughtfully he pulled at his
lower lip as he turned away.

Dinner was served to the three of them in the
dining-room, and Irene certainly did justice to the
well cooked meal. Later they sat before a small log
fire and Mrs Marron began to talk of the history of
the island; she had a racy way of explaining and des-
cribing things and the other two listened intently.
Irene knew she would enjoy taking dictation from
this woman; the subjects would be varied and would
not be dry. At times her expressions were caustic
and the two young people would smile and more
than once they exchanged understanding glances.
Finally Mrs Marron glanced at her watch.

'Last night I was plotting out all I intended writing to the Minister about the project suggested in
the vicinity of the gorge——' Alex raised his head
quickly and she nodded at him. 'Yes—the one
Twilight Constructions are so keen about. What's
been suggested for that area must not be allowed
to eventuate! I'll have the whole thing squashed.'
Her hand came down hard on the arm of her chair,
her voice deepened and grew harsh and Irene looked
at her in surprise. 'I will complete these notes and
tomorrow, after we've returned from our drive when
I've had another look at the place, we'll get down to
business in earnest.' She smiled at her new secretary.
'You've had a long and I hope exciting day, so I

think you should go to bed in good time.'

Alex stood up. 'Is that a hint for Irene to go now?'

'It is. I want her as fresh as a daisy in the morning.' The chair was turned towards the door and Lulu immediately moved to walk beside it. 'Goodnight, my dear. If you find you haven't everything you need tell Netta and she'll attend to it. Alex, can you spare me a few minutes, please?'

Irene was only sleepy with the warmth of the fire, not physically tired, and she opened the window in her room to look up at the starlit sky through the branches of the apple tree. The world was at peace in this lovely spot and she gave a deep sigh of content as she laid her chin on her crossed arms and gazed into the night. There were no lights, no sounds to break the comforting stillness and as she looked up at the stars she felt a gradual relaxation of her body. Finally she turned, drew the curtains and was starting to undress in the dark when there was a faint tap on the half open window.

'Irene? Are you asleep already? Irene?' The whisper drifted into the room and pulling her frock down over her shoulders she pulled the curtains slowly back. 'It's me, Alex——'

'I guessed that,' she breathed. 'What's the matter?' Their faces almost touched as she leaned out. 'Oh!'

'I didn't mean to startle you, but I had a thought.' There was a laugh in his voice.

'Have you indeed!'

'It was a thought about the car, but when you're so close to me and I can feel your soft breath on my cheek I could think of many other things,' he murmured.

'The car?' Seriousness replaced the mirth in her voice. 'What's wrong?'

'Mum used to be a very good driver and she expects everyone to have the same standard of proficiency as she had. I've been wondering if you've ever driven one like ours. If you haven't it would be as well to try it out before you go with her in the morning.'

'Now?'

Alex nodded. 'I'll come with you and show you how everything works and you could drive around until you get the feel of it. I'd hate you to fluff out on your test tomorrow.'

'I would hate that too,' was the quiet admission. 'But your mother would hear us.'

'I often get night calls. It's not at all unusual for me to drive away at any hour. She was reading when I left her, but Netta was on her way to help get her into bed. If I get the car out and meet you down the road in about fifteen minutes——'

She hesitated. 'It seems rather underhand and deceitful.'

'First impressions count a lot with my parent.'

She glanced over his shoulder through the branches of the tree towards the countryside hidden now in the darkness. Only a few hours ago she had seen it for the first time and now she had no wish to leave it, for there was a feeling of tranquillity in the very air. Something stirred within her, something which had been dormant ever since she had left the old home, the something which had made her father smile at her, call her his 'Tomboy Joe' and ruffle her hair as she danced along beside him. She nodded, and her head was so close to his that Alex could feel her hair against his cheek.

'But I'll have to go through the house.'

'Oh, no! You simply climb out of the window! What could be more convenient? Both Carl and I did it often when we were in our teens and had been sent to our respective rooms as a punishment for something or other. I'll meet you down by the hedge —keep to the right when you come out and you'll miss Netta's window and Brutus won't hear you. He pretends he's deaf, but it's amazing what he can hear when he wants and you don't! Fifteen minutes from now,' he whispered, and vanished into the darkness.

Irene turned back into the room; she was trembling a little, but whether it was excitement or not she did not know. Nothing could be more different from what it had been twenty-four hours ago! As she slipped a dark coat over her shoulders she thought of her room at the flat; if she had climbed out of the window there she would have been in a cul-de-sac, with buildings all around, with the whine of traffic on the main road and the flashing of neon lights at the corner advertising 'Bert's Hamburgers'.

'I would never have dared to climb out of that window,' she informed herself as she scrambled over the sill and dropped on to the grass which grew up to the walls. It was a longer drop than she had thought and for a moment she wondered how she would get back in again. Silently she moved along to the right; there were other windows and she ducked her head as she passed them, but they were all in darkness. Then more lawn and trees and beyond that what she called the thicket and Alex the hedge. As she reached it the car, with only its side lights on, came to a silent stop beside her, the door was opened and within moments they were driving down the white road.

CHAPTER 4

'You're shivering! or trembling. Which?'

'I don't know,' Irene admitted. 'It's years since I did anything like this!'

Alex raised his eyebrows. 'So you've climbed out of windows before?'

'And gone swimming in the dam in the moonlight. And ridden over paddocks with my brother when everyone else was asleep. Oh, yes, I had my moments when I was young!'

He gave a hoot of delighted laughter. 'Listen to her! Ah, youth! I really go for someone who doesn't always conform to the rules. Honey, I think when I get to know you better and hear more of your past I'm going to fall in love with you.'

'Not until you've shown me how to drive this contraption, please.' Her tone of voice was as light as his and she had the same feeling of comradeship as she had had with her brother.

The car stopped and he opened the door. 'Move over and we'll start the first lesson.'

He was patient and understanding. The seat had to be moved forward and the safety belts adjusted, and he remarked on how tiny she looked behind the wheel. He made her start, stop and reverse, and when he felt she understood the gears and was becoming used to the pedals on the floor he encouraged her to pick up speed. There was no other traffic on the roads and Irene gradually relaxed and found pleasure in the way she could handle it. The darkness shut them in. Black half seen things slipped by, a blur that was a house, a long smudge that was a line of trees, a high hedge which Alex informed her was hawthorn towered above the car as they sped along. Then a glint of water from a river and she felt very thankful to have been given this chance of becoming used to the car before driving Mrs Marron out for the first time. Alex sat back and relaxed, there was a smile on his face.

'You'll do,' he said quietly. 'You'll come through with flying colours, and if you go to the gorge tomorrow you'll be even more used to it before driving through traffic.'

'I'm very grateful, Alex.'

'Think nothing of it. There's nothing I enjoy more than driving through the night with an attractive girl by my side. You've brought a touch of spice and enchantment into my narrow life. Let's elope!'

Irene laughed. 'We wouldn't get far. The petrol gauge shows empty.'

'There'll be sufficient to get us home.' He did not sound concerned.

The car glided to a standstill about a quarter of a mile from the house. Irene switched off the ignition, yawned as she unfastened the safety belt and opened the door. 'We walk, I presume?'

'And I'll have to walk back with a can of petrol—someone might ring during the night and want me urgently.' He yawned. 'And if we left the car here someone might ask why——'

'There's another car coming. Who's driving out here at this time of night?'

'Time of morning, it's well turned twelve. Maybe someone with a sick animal.'

They waited beside the car. The headlights were shining on them as the other drew nearer, it slowed and came to a stop, the driver alighted and moved in front of the lights. Irene caught her breath and her face lost its colour as she recognised the tall figure. Alex blinked.

'Carl! I thought you weren't coming home until the weekend!'

'I changed my mind,' the crisp voice announced. 'I see you arrived safely, Miss Peterson—this afternoon, wasn't it?' She felt like a schoolgirl caught out in some childish prank and wished she could fade out of sight behind the nearest tree. 'Been out for the evening?'

The tone of his voice as he looked at them both made her bite her lips, but it certainly did not put his cousin out of countenance. He merely smiled and said, 'No, we went for a driving lesson.'

'I was informed that Miss Peterson *could* drive.'

'And so she can. But this car, you'll remember, was bought for one person for one purpose. And I didn't want Irene to be sent packing because she didn't reach my mother's high standard. Smooth stops, no grating of gears—you know.' Alex looked at him seriously.

'Yes,' agreed Carl thoughtfully, glancing from his face to that of the girl. 'I know. I'm sorry, Miss Peterson, I thought my charming cousin had prevailed upon you to drive with him in the moonlight.'

'There isn't any,' pointed out Alex. 'We've been in the dark.'

'Oh, Alex!' she breathed.

'And we ran out of petrol nearly at the front door. I certainly didn't plan it right, did I?' he asked dolefully, and Carl laughed.

'You're incorrigible, Alex. I presume your mother doesn't know about this?'

'Of course not! Irene slipped out at my invitation and insistence and since then has been getting the feel of the thing. She'll have nothing to fear from now on.'

'I'm very glad to hear it. In that case I'd better take you back, Miss Peterson, and then I'll return with some petrol for you——'

'If you don't the whole heinous plot will be exposed,' commented his cousin, leaning back against the car and lighting a cigarette.

In silence Irene moved to the other car, and when Carl opened the door she slipped into the seat and tried her best to look inconspicuous. It was a fine beginning, she thought unhappily, to be caught out on her first night here in an escapade she was convinced Mrs Marron would not find at all amusing. Carl did not speak; he dimmed the lights and drove round to the back of the house where the car came to a silent stop near one of the garages. Turning in his seat, he asked,

'Did you use the front door?'

'I came out through my bedroom window,' she said hesitantly but truthfully, and did not turn her head, so she did not see the smile which crossed his face.

'In that case I shall have to help you.'

'I can manage,' she said quickly.

'I very much doubt it. You're so small, and the window must be at least four feet from the ground—if you start scratching about trying to find a foothold on the bricks Brutus is sure to hear you and then Netta will put her head out of the window and demand to know what's going on. She's very narrow-minded in some respects,' he added.

Irene wondered despairingly if he was annoyed by what she had done and felt some excuse must be made. 'It was because of tomorrow, you see. Mrs Marron wants me to drive her to a gorge somewhere.' There was a muttered exclamation and for the first time Irene stole a glance at his face, but he said nothing and she went on quickly, 'Alex, as he told you, didn't want me to make any mistakes, neither did I want to spoil anything. Oh, Mr Morgan, I like it here, it's so peaceful and lovely, the kind of place where I could be really happy.'

'And it has trees,' he murmured. 'I understand. But really it has nothing to do with me now. You're in my aunt's employ, not mine. Rest assured, neither Alex nor I will ever say anything about this. So I'd better get you back into your own room.'

His hand was on her arm as he guided her towards the darkened house, their footsteps deadened by the soft grass, and when they reached the window, recognisable by the apple tree, she realised that she would not have been able to clamber in without some assistance. She wished it was Alex standing beside her; he would have seen some humour in this and they would have stifled their laughter as he helped her in over the sill. Carl heaved as though she was a sack of potatoes, she bumped her knees against the wall, the branches of the tree scratched her arms and she was dropped on to the carpet with a slight thump.

'Thank you,' she whispered as she turned round. He gave a nonchalant wave and moved into the night, and Irene sat on the edge of the bed wondering whether to laugh or cry, then she put her hands over her face and did both.

Very much to her surprise she felt and looked as fresh as a daisy, as Mrs Marron had wished her to be when she went along to breakfast the following morning. She had slept without moving or dreaming until Netta had come in with a cup of tea and the abrupt remark, 'Breakfast will be in half an hour.'

For just a moment as she looked around Irene wondered where she was, and as soon as the door closed behind the housekeeper she was out of bed peering through the window to make sure the apple tree had not vanished. As other memories flooded back she glanced ruefully at the faint scratches on her arms and a faint flush spread over her cheeks as she remembered the strength in Carl's arms as he lifted her up to enable her to scramble through the window.

To her relief he was not in the dining-room when she went in. No one else was there either, but the front door was open and she heard Mrs Marron talking to the dogs. Both the labrador and the little mongrel gave her a friendly welcome and Mrs Marron looked approvingly at her as she joined her.

'Evidently you slept well,' she observed.

'I did,' the girl smiled as she looked round and sniffed the cool clear air with appreciation. 'What a lovely morning, and what a lovely garden.'

'I hope you'll like living here.' The wheelchair moved forward. 'There's Netta, so breakfast will be ready. Then we'll head towards the peak you mentioned yesterday—I have a busy day ahead and have decided to take lunch. Please take along all the things you'll need, books, pencils and whatever.' And then, on their return, she would know just how well this girl performed her duties.

Alex followed them into the dining-room, greeting his mother with a pat on the head as he walked behind her chair and looking at Irene with great seriousness as he enquired if she had had a good night. She wondered if he would mention that his cousin had arrived home, but as the meal progressed it was obvious he had no intention of doing any such thing. Instead he told them about Cinderella and her family and of the heartbreaking expression in

59

the eyes of the shaggy dog. Irene hoped she would have the chance of seeing the piglets and the rest of his menagerie before very long, but realised it would be best to wait until Mrs Marron suggested she went to the kennels or until she had some free time.

The door opened again and without glancing round she knew Carl had made his appearance, for his aunt looked both pleased and startled as he went immediately to her side and kissed her gently on the cheek.

'When did you arrive? We didn't expect you for another few days.' She turned her head and raised one hand to touch his face.

'I caught the last plane and as my car was in the usual garage I naturally drove straight home. And how are you, Miss Peterson?' He glanced across the table. 'It's nice to see you again too. I hope you had a good trip over.'

'I did, thank you.' The words sounded prim and she concentrated all her attention on spreading a piece of toast with honey.

'And Alex!' Carl sounded almost startled as he looked at his cousin. 'I thought you would have been down amongst those noisy beasts. Something must have upset them—the dogs are barking their heads off, there are pigs squealing, calves crying out for their mothers——'

'Don't make it sound as though they're badly neglected,' cried Alex. 'The little dears have had food, water and my undivided attention for the past hour. I hope you told Netta you're home, since I appear to have eaten the last of the toast.'

'Netta will be bringing in my breakfast any moment now.' Carl sat down, removed the large bowl of red and white dahlias towards the end of the table, and Irene discovered he was sitting exactly opposite to her.

'There you are, Carl, you'll enjoy this. All nice and hot it is too!' A plump arm stretched over his shoulder and Netta's ample bosom touched his head as she placed a well-filled plate before him. Alex glanced at Irene as though he was silently inviting her to share a memory and she snatched at her table napkin and coughed into it, turning her head away so that she could no longer see his laughing eyes.

'I'm sorry,' she apologised, wiping her eyes as Netta moved round the table.

'Did something get in the way?' asked her tormentor innocently, and she nodded, mutely begging him to change the subject. Mrs Marron obliged.

'Why did you decide to come home so much earlier?' she asked her nephew.

'I'd completed all I had to do in Sydney, enjoyed a few rounds of golf and decided there was too much work waiting for me over here.'

'Such as?' Her voice had an edge to it.

Carl looked at her with rather an odd smile. 'All the usual things. What else?'

She shrugged her shoulders, confident he would not trouble her today, as he knew nothing of her plan to visit the gorge or of the arrangements she had made to meet various people there. And for obvious reasons nothing had been publicised.

'But I'm not in such a hurry,' he added. 'Is there anywhere I can drive you? Or anything else I can do?'

'Thank you, no. Irene is going with me, we have to become better acquainted and there's much we have to discuss. St Valentine's Peak appealed to her when she glimpsed it for the first time yesterday——'

'I hope she sees peaks much higher than that during her stay with us.' He made it sound, thought Irene, as though he was confident she would be here for a very long time.

'She will,' promised Alex, draining the last of the coffee in his cup and standing up. 'I shall take her myself in the hours off my mother allows her.' There was another affectionate pat on his mother's head as he moved behind her chair. 'I can't spend my time gossiping about mountains over the breakfast table, I have many things to do. See you all later!'

With that he was gone and after a few minutes the din from the kennels died away.

'Which way do you intend driving?' asked Carl casually, and his aunt answered in the same tone of voice.

'To Riana, Hampshire, and back through Burnie.'

'A very nice round trip,' he nodded agreeably.

'And I think we'll go now.' Mrs Marron spun her chair away from the table. 'Sometimes the weather can change very quickly, though it looks settled enough at the moment.'

Irene sensed a feeling of aggression between aunt and nephew; it was not too apparent but was definitely there. With a faint smile at the man still sitting at the table she followed Mrs Marron from the room, and Carl stared thoughtfully out of the window at the brilliant green of the lawn. It had been a very casual conversation and nothing had been given away; if it had not been for Irene's remark as he escorted her across the lawn the night before, he would have known nothing about the proposed visit to the gorge. It was as well he had returned sooner than anticipated.

Netta had packed a picnic lunch and Irene, going into the comfortable study, collected shorthand books, pencils and a few other things she noticed and thrust them all into the shoulder-bag which was large and of stiff leather, she could place a book on it and write with ease even when standing. Feeling quite confident of coping with anything that came along, she went for her coat and joined Mrs Marron by the car which Alex had left conveniently at the front gate.

'Have you ever driven one of this make before?' asked the elder woman suddenly, and the girl, as she opened the door and Lulu jumped in, kept her face averted as she answered truthfully, 'Only once.'

'Do you feel you can manage it?'

The brown head was nodded energetically and she was thankful to be spared any further questions as Netta assisted her beloved mistress. Irene stood near the door watching every move that was made, for there could possibly come a time when she would have to place the chair up against the wide open door and hold it steady as Mrs Marron's strong arms supported the weight of her body for the brief moment as she swung herself on to the car seat. Netta pushed the chair to one side and leaned in to help her into a more comfortable position.

'And there's your cushions, and be sure to get someone to help if you will insist on getting out. You can hold court here just as well as on the outside! That lass isn't strong enough to help——' she added under her breath as she folded the chair and beckoned rather imperiously to Irene to open the boot where it was stowed away.

From the dining-room window Carl watched. He knew better than to go out with offers of assistance when Netta was within call and wondered what his aunt would do if her companion of so many years was taken ill. He saw Irene go round to the driver's side, watched as she adjusted the seat and the safety belt, heard the instant purr of the engine as she switched on and within a moment the car was moving from the gate. He nodded to himself at the smooth start and went into Alex's room where there was an extension and shut the door quietly behind him before picking up the phone.

Alex was watching and waiting, sitting astride a gate, the leads of four dogs held firmly in his fingers. He waved a handkerchief wildly and enthusiastically as though they were passing royalty, thought Irene with a smile, and his mother waved back graciously and laughed at the antics of the dogs as they tangled themselves round his legs and the gate-post. She was so thankful her son was a veterinary surgeon and had no interest in real estate or development programmes.

This was something she had been dreading, having a new driver behind the wheel. She was one of those people who, having been an excellent driver herself, always felt nervous with anyone else, and none of the other girls had given her any feeling of confidence. As she gave instructions about turning this way or that she felt some of the tenseness leave her and more than once told Irene to stop so she could point out places along the magnificent panoramas of coastline, farmlands and mountains. Rivers were crossed and the peak which the girl had seen from her bedroom stood up closely and clearly against the blue sky; when she remarked upon the clarity of the air Mrs Marron answered, rather superciliously, 'No pollution!'

The road petered out to a mere track and mentally Irene wholeheartedly thanked Alex for giving her the opportunity of becoming used to the car, for now she could concentrate her whole attention on the ruts, potholes and large puddles. She wished she could linger, for the track appeared to run along the top of a ridge and there were other peaks away in the distance which appeared much higher than that of St Valentine. Suddenly they reached a tar-sealed road and she was told to turn left.

The gorge was unexpected. The trees were very

tall and thick and their branches met over the road which dropped suddenly in a series of twists and turns towards a bridge which crossed a wide foaming river. Huge rocks were scattered along the river banks and the first impression was of a wild beauty such as she had never seen before. She was instructed to pull off the road under the trees where many wheel tracks showed that it was a popular place for sightseeing and picnics. Numerous other cars were already there and men were standing about in groups, some talking earnestly together, others craning their necks to look up at the trees and the rock-stubbed slopes. Many moved forward as the car came to a standstill.

'Your chair?' asked Irene over her shoulder, and the other woman nodded. Lulu was first out and waited patiently until Mrs Marron was settled with the aid of a strong arm belonging to a man who had obviously assisted in this way before. Introductions followed; many were well-known names and a few faces were familiar as Irene had seen them being interviewed on television. Not knowing exactly what was required of her, she stood listening intently to the conversation. Mrs Marron was at ease and laughing at various remarks passed between the men in the surrounding group, then her voice changed suddenly and became tense as she looked beyond those nearest to her to meet the eyes of a man watching from beneath the thick canopy of leaves nearby.

'And why did you come here today?' she called

sharply, and the others around her moved aside as the man sauntered leisurely towards her.

'Because, very naturally, I'm interested in what may be the outcome of the meeting,' he said mildly.

'How did you know the meeting was to take place?' she snapped.

'It was fairly common knowledge, Mrs Marron. It's not, after all, a private matter between yourself and these gentlemen. It concerns everyone.'

'How right you are!' Her voice was bitingly cold. 'Everyone who is interested in keeping beauty spots such as this in their natural state and out of the hands of so-called developers. You would spoil them all if you had your way.'

The wheelchair moved forward quickly, almost knocking down a rotund gentleman of the Senate who was peering shortsightedly at the bark of the nearest tree. The man to whom Mrs Marron had been so blunt glanced at Irene and slightly shrugged his shoulders.

'I haven't seen you before,' he remarked, moving to her side. 'Are you interested in conservation too?'

'As much as most people these days, I think,' she smiled. 'I'm Mrs Marron's secretary.' She glanced towards where the chair was now surrounded by at least a dozen men and wondered if she should be there to take down all that was being said.

'These are only the preliminaries, the skirmishes,' the man informed her. 'Do you live near here?'

'I arrived in Tasmania only yesterday.' There was a look in her eyes which he found hard to define, almost one of mischief. His eyebrows went up in surprise.

'And you're on the job already!'

'Why, yes, that's what I came for. I think I'd better join them.'

Neal Sheldon watched her walk across the grass, thinking Carl's description of her had been very accurate. She was petite and moved with an unusual grace, and she was conscientious, for she had withdrawn a notebook from the shoulder bag and was already making notes of all that was being said. He joined the party, standing behind the wheelchair and, using his own expression, with his ears pinned well back.

Irene learnt much that lovely day as she went with the crowd and studied trees, rock formations and the swirling restless river. She was filled with indignation as she realised that the people gathered here were fighting a proposal to open this land for development; there was mention of a motel on top of the gorge, built so that the occupants could gaze down towards the river, which meant the clearing of hundreds of trees. All the time her pencil moved swiftly across the lines; she was determined that in the evening she would be able to read back every word spoken and every argument both for and against, and she would definitely be among those who were against.

Lunch was partaken of under the trees and afterwards the party moved over the bridge to the other side of the river, and Neal Sheldon was always on the fringe of it. He had excellent hearing and would report all the objections which were being lodged by this gathering and which would have to be overcome to enable them to proceed with the project Carl and his friends had in mind.

The discussion came to an end at last. Mrs Marron was settled into the car, but their departure was delayed when it was discovered that Lulu was not with them. She was seen on the far side of the river, whining and whimpering because she was afraid to try to swim across, and Irene ran back over the bridge, returning with the trembling dog in her arms and murmuring words of comfort. Mrs Marron watched with a contented smile.

'We'll return by the main road,' she said. By doing so she would be making the trip she had described to Carl that morning, although she knew it would not be long before he was informed of all that had transpired at the gorge.

She stared unseeingly at the passing landscape, wondering how Neal Sheldon had managed to discover the time and date of the meeting when it had been arranged at very short notice. Her nephew could have had no inkling of it, for he had arrived back so late the night before and there had been no phone calls either to Glendene or from it before her departure after breakfast. She was fond of her sister's only child, but that did not mean she agreed with him in all he said, did or planned to do. And this latest plan of his must be stopped at all costs; she *would* stop it, for she could be just as ruthless as he was. Did they not both come from the same family? And had not the early Marrons and Morgans fought this strange land from the time they arrived in the late eighteenth century, fought to make it what it was today, and one of them at least would fight on to preserve the heritage their ancestors had given them.

'Irene?' The girl lifted her head at the softly spoken word. 'I'm sure there's no need for me to say that anything you hear, or write in letters and articles to my supporters, is all confidential——'

Irene stiffened and she interrupted, something she had never done before. 'Mrs Marron, I worked for years in a solicitor's office and I never betrayed a confidence!' There was a reprimand in the trembling voice. 'Of course I wouldn't dream of divulging your affairs or discussing my work with anyone!'

A thin hand reached out and touched the rigid shoulder. 'I should have had more sense than to say such a thing. My apologies.'

Irene nodded and changed the subject by asking which fork in the road she was to take. They reached the coast again and she was directed through the busy town of Burnie with the promise to come back again in the very near future, as there was much to see which was of great interest, especially to people from the mainland. She smiled at the slight inference in the cultured voice, as though the mainlanders were a race apart. And thinking it over, she supposed they were!

CHAPTER 5

To make up for what she realised was lack of tact on her part Mrs Marron suggested that they called on their way home to see Alex at his surgery. No, she would not get out of the car, she stated as they stopped at the place indicated; she had been many times before and as there was no particular hurry, Irene could go and listen to all the enthusiastic explanations of what he had, why he had it and what he did with it.

'Walk straight in,' she advised, and the girl did so. There was a small waiting room which contained a desk and a filing cabinet, there was also a large tank of fish along one wall, and Irene noticed with a smile that there were no carpets on the floor and no magazines in racks, such as were found in doctors' surgeries. She could imagine people sitting in the chairs, nursing their pets and exchanging confidences about what they thought was wrong and what amusing antics they got up to when they were well.

The door facing her was opened and Alex, in a white coat, popped his head out.

'Why, Irene!' There was great delight in his voice as he hurried forward. 'I thought I had a patient and instead I find you! This is a wonderful surprise—how did you know I was here?'

'Your mother——'

'There's nothing wrong, is there?' His expression and his voice changed immediately and she reassured him swiftly.

'Nothing at all. We're on our way back and it was suggested that I might like to see your surgery.'

'And you did like?'

'Of course!'

He eyed her with unconcealed admiration. 'There must be something extraordinary about you! I knew it as soon as I met you yesterday, of course, but for my mother to discover it so soon amazes me! Never before has she suggested that any of the many damsels she's had as secretaries visit me here. Come in, come in.'

The second room was fitted like a surgery and had a strong smell of disinfectant. There were glass-fronted cupboards containing bottles, jars and canisters, trays of instruments and a small sterilizer bubbled gently to itself in a corner near what was obviously an examination table. There were straps hanging down from this and Alex confirmed her suspicion that they were to hold down some of his patients.

'You have no idea how awkward some of them can be,' he smiled at her. 'Have you had a good day, and did you drive the car in the manner to which it's become accustomed to be driven?'

'There were no comments passed,' she admitted.

'In that case our little subterfuge succeeded. And no one will ever know.'

'There's Mr Morgan——'

'Mr Morgan,' he mimicked her. 'Why is he addressed so and I'm only Alex?'

She lowered her eyes. 'If you would prefer it, Mr Marron——'

'Don't stand there so demurely, looking like a little girl waiting to be kissed. If you don't want me to do just that you'd better answer my question.'

'Well, he's different from you. He's older,' Irene cried quickly, and his shout of delighted laughter was heard by his mother sitting in the car outside. She smiled at the sound of it as her fingers gently stroked the soft fur under Lulu's chin. 'How old do you think he is?'

'I don't really know.' Now she looked confused and no longer demure. 'And I don't really care!'

'For your information, he'll be thirty at the end of this year. But his wealth and position, apart from his great age, doesn't mean you shouldn't call him Carl. Especially when at Glendene, he's merely my cousin. And you need never worry that he'll spill the beans or inform the world in general of our escapade last night. He keeps his own counsel—a clam has nothing on him at times.' He tucked his hand through her arm. 'Forget Carl and look at what arrived in here a couple of hours ago. It's to be an extra-special guest of mine for the next week.'

Tiptoeing with exaggerated caution across the room, he waved towards an old shoe box, and Irene moved forward wondering what it could contain. Certainly not piglets! She bent over and Alex chuckled with delight as he watched her expression change.

'It *looks* like a penguin,' she murmured in disbelief.

'And you're right. It's a fairy penguin, the smallest of the flightless sea birds, and it was found by a young friend of mine on Bruny Island a couple of weeks ago. It was nearly dead when he brought it to me, but between us we've managed to keep it alive. I've had little to do with the species before and feeding it has been a headache. Martin is going away for a week and I've been requested to take it home with me and act as its foster-parent.'

'And it goes into the kitchen, alongside a box of kittens with Netta looking after it,' she hazarded a guess.

Alex nodded. 'You can take it back with you if you're going now. I've one or two calls to make and there's someone I must see——'

'I thought I'd become the one love of your life!' Irene sighed deeply.

'Oh, you are. But I can't drop all the others immediately, surely you understand that?' He turned away from her and she glanced fleetingly at his face. All the laughter had gone from his eyes and he looked older and different. 'Let's take this out to the car.'

Mrs Marron raised her eyebrows when she saw the box and sighed when her son handed it to her with instructions not to tip it upside down. Lulu sniffed inquisitively, but like her mistress she had become used to strange things and settled back on the rug.

'And what's Netta going to say about this?' Mrs Marron demanded. 'It's a new one to her!'

'All the things she's said before.' There was total unconcern in his voice. 'It's only until I get home, then I'll put it in a more suitable place—penguins were not intended to live in kitchens. Had a good day, Mum? Will things turn out as you hope they will?'

She frowned as she remembered Neal Sheldon watching and listening from the edge of the crowd and shrugged her shoulders.

'Like the outcome of this little sea creature's life, it's uncertain what will happen.'

'Tough luck.' He still looked rather tight around the mouth, thought Irene wonderingly. 'I won't be in for dinner,' he added, and watched with approval as the car moved off into the traffic.

Mrs Marron was preoccupied during dinner and later when they went into the study she sat before the fire and stared into it, then she raised her head.

'What notes did you manage to take down, Irene?'

'Quite a lot. I only hope I have what you need.' Her fingers flicked the pages of the shorthand book. 'Shall I read them to you?'

'Please.'

The soft voice was clear and distinct and as page after page was turned over Mrs Marron listened in amazement. The girl was a wonder—everything which had been said, relevant or irrelevant, by various members of different organisations was being repeated, and by closing her eyes she could visualise the places, the paths, even the very rocks to which they referred. Irene reached the last page, put down the book and glanced anxiously across the lovely room.

'Was that what you wanted?'

With a start the other came back to her surroundings. 'What I wanted! It's exactly what I wanted, and more than I ever expected. You've caught the whole essence of the day for me. I could picture the prima donna, the one with the high squeaky voice and the bald head—you must remember him, for he could be heard above everyone else, hence his nickname, telling Sir Angus why his ideas should be accepted and not those of the gentleman of opposition. If I could hear again the part about the water flow?'

'It wouldn't take me long to type it out for you. The written word is easier to memorise than the spoken one.'

'How right you are, thank you.' Mrs Marron smiled, picked up her own book of notes and began to read through them, but within ten minutes she knew she would have to put them down and go to bed. The dreadful feeling of lassitude was creeping over her, a legacy of the accident when her brain felt numb and she did not feel to have an ounce of strength left in her body. It would pass as it always did after a couple of tablets prescribed by her doctor and a good night's sleep. She pressed the bell handy to her chair and within seconds Netta was in the room. She took one look at Mrs Marron and glanced across at the bent head behind the desk suspiciously, wondering if she had upset her.

'It's just the usual,' murmured Mrs Marron. 'Nothing to worry about. I think I'll leave you to it, Irene, if you don't mind continuing with the typing?'

'Not at all,' the girl murmured without looking up, and if she had dared Netta would have slammed the door behind her as she wheeled the chair from the room.

Irene's fingers stopped for a moment as she remembered what Carl had said during the interview in Sydney. Now this was the beginning and if it continued in the same way she would be the happiest person in Tasmania. Nothing, she thought, must jeopardise her position in this household, not when it included days spent among tall trees with a foaming river making conversation impossible when standing on its banks. Or the sight of a very tiny helpless fairy penguin in an old shoe box. She smiled to herself as she bent over the typewriter, heedless of the passing of time.

'I did warn you this would happen, didn't I?' asked a voice quietly, and she looked up with a startled expression on her face.

'Oh, I didn't hear you. And I don't mind this at all.'

'Where is Aunt Kate?'

'She went out with Netta a while ago,' she answered, vague as to how long it was since she had been left alone. 'Perhaps she was tired.'

Carl nodded. 'Maybe, if she's been out all day. She

77

must have done a lot of dictating.' He glanced down at the pile of papers beside the typewriter as he moved to the desk. 'Finding it interesting?'

'Very,' she smiled. 'There, that's the last page.'

'And about time, it's turned half past ten.' Moving to her side, he watched as she pulled the sheets from the carriage; he could see nothing of what was typed on it, for Irene laid a blank sheet over the top, bunched them neatly together and put them into a drawer. Then she leaned back in the chair and stretched.

'Did you enjoy the run? Where did you get to?' He sounded interested as he perched upon the edge of the desk and looked down at her.

'I couldn't tell you the names of the places we went through, I simply followed directions and loved every minute of it. Oh, it was beautiful,' she went on dreamily. 'I've never seen so many green paddocks, such fat cattle, lovely vistas and so many trees! And the trip along the coastline made me want to get out and explore every little bay and cove.'

She had given nothing away, he thought with an inward laugh. 'And did you notice the railway line?'

'Following every beach and headland——'

'And wandering through cuttings in the rocks on the water's edge.'

'At times it was almost on the sand,' her eyes opened wide with delight. 'Then we called to see Alex at his surgery and brought back a little penguin with us.'

'I've seen it. It's still in the kitchen.'

'So he hasn't come back yet?'

'He'll be out with one of his numerous girl-friends,' he answered casually. 'A very popular young man, my cousin. I'd advise you not to take him seriously.'

'And why should I do that? I met him yesterday for the first time.' Was it only yesterday? So much seemed to have happened since the hour of her arrival and she felt so much more at home in this lovely house.

'The only thing Alex takes seriously is his work. The rest of the world and all mankind are a joke to him.'

Irene remembered the look which had crossed his cousin's face and knew Carl was wrong, very wrong, in his interpretation of the other's attitude to life. Alex would be more understanding than his cousin, he would see things in their correct perspective and be more gentle, partly because it was his nature to be that way and partly because he needed all those things in his work, when dealing with dumb animals who could not explain to him their pain and fright. She looked up to see the rugged face with the keen eyes smiling at her. He was relaxed and friendly, different altogether from the man she had met in the motel.

'Last night you went for a drive with him—oh, I know the reason and it evidently paid off. Tonight may I suggest a walk with me to clear away any cob-webs? You'll sleep better afterwards if you've been typing all evening. It's a beautiful night,' he murmured, and put his hand on the back of her chair.

It was useless to glance at her watch and say it was getting late, and weakly Irene stood up knowing she had no desire to argue against the idea.

'You'll need a coat,' he added.

Brutus heard Carl's voice, he heard the light feet of the girl go along the hall and return and decided to investigate. With his nose he opened the kitchen door a little wider to enable him to get his bulky body through and upon discovering they were going out of the front door he dashed after them. In his enthusiasm he brushed against Irene and nearly knocked her over. Carl's arm went round her to steady her and at his touch she felt a warmth creep over her.

'Stupid dog!' he grumbled. 'He doesn't get out as often as he should, Netta isn't one for walking and he's getting as fat as she is!'

Brutus was trying to give an imitation of a playful puppy and they both had to laugh at his antics as they walked over the lawn away from the house. It was a beautiful night, still and very cool, with the sky so clear that Irene felt she could, with the aid of a long ladder, pick stars as she would flowers, and thought what a beautiful necklace they would make. With Alex she would have shared the idiotic thought, but Carl was of a different mould and she did not want him to think she was slightly crazy. So she walked beside him in silence.

Carl glanced down at her. How different from

some of the others who had been to Glendene! She was quiet and efficient, but he had a shrewd idea, from the way she had spoken to Alex and of the sudden gleam of mischief which could come into her eyes, that once her reserve had been broken through she would be an amusing and delightful companion. He hoped so for Aunt Kate's sake as she deserved the best of everything, and that included secretaries, after the blow fate had dealt her on that sunny morning a few years ago. But he did wish his aunt would not dabble in this conservation business or take it so seriously; she would be much better employed with her short stories, which were a delight, and her articles, so varied and knowledgeable, for the magazines and newspapers. Neal Sheldon, when he had phoned and given him the results of the day's discussions, was pessimistic about the outcome as it concerned their plans. Mrs Marron, he complained, had some very forceful arguments and had been listened to with close attention by those who had been at the gorge, and the names he had mentioned had made Carl frown. Aunt Kate would be taking up politics next!

Within the next week or so a decision would be arrived at by the powers that be and he wanted to know what it was before it was made public. Once again he glanced down at the slim figure by his side.

'Did Alex tell you my home is similar to this?' he asked idly. 'As a matter of fact it's older and has quite a history.'

'He did mention it,' Irene agreed. 'And also said

it was too big for one bloke on his own.'

'Me being the bloke?' he laughed. 'It's larger than Glendene. In the days when the island colony was young, people had large families and needed the space. Land was cheap, so was labour, and the Morgans, until the last two generations, had umpteen children and plenty of room for them. Many died in their infancy in those days and others began to drift away from the land, some went to the mainland, some overseas. Gradually the large properties were broken up—we have quite a few thousand acres less now than the family had fifty years ago. My mother is at present visiting many relatives in England. I was her only child and so I'm the last of the line as regards Tarrentall.'

'Tarrentall? What a delightful name!'

'It's a delightful place. As the crow flies it's not so far from here, but to go by road it's many miles with three rivers to cross, including the Forth. Next time I go over there would you like to come with me? I would like you to see it.'

She replied without hesitation. 'When Mrs Marron can spare me for a while I would like to, but I have an idea we're going to be busy for the next week or so.' He raised his eyebrows at that remark. 'Doesn't anyone live there?' asked Irene, reverting back to the original subject.

'A couple of men who attend to the stock. There are pedigree Jerseys and Guernseys, but I'm afraid I haven't the time to spare to be very interested in them. Alex is the one who keeps an eye on the place and buys and sells stock when he thinks fit and at his discretion. It's more in his line than mine.'

She felt a little disappointed at his lack of interest in his own property and wondered if he would think her presumptuous if she enquired what line he preferred, and waited, hoping he would volunteer the information. No one else had told her what Carl did for a living. But Brutus came bounding up to them with a large stick in his mouth which he laid at Carl's feet and waited, his tail wagging furiously with anticipation.

'He's gone mad!' muttered Carl. 'Netta really will have to get off her big behind and take him out more often.'

'I'd do that willingly, if she wouldn't mind.'

'You'd better ask her first,' he remarked, throwing the stick across the lawn, and Irene nodded seriously.

'I wouldn't like to tread on Netta's toes.' She hesitated. 'She gives me the impression of loving you all and Glendene so much——'

'That she's become possessive,' Carl finished the sentence for her. 'How right you are! But what Aunt Kate would do without her none of us know.'

Netta watched from her window as they returned slowly to the house. She had heard the deep bark of her dog and got up to discover him nudging against the girl, trying to push the stick he carried into her hands. She saw Carl bend his head down towards the brown curly one and heard a faint laugh and she compressed her lips. Alex was not the only one who could be attentive and charming, though with him it was natural and not put on for some purpose or another. She remembered occasions in Carl's youth, when he had used to the utmost the captivating wiles necessary to get what he wanted from his mother, his aunt and herself.

He stopped on the front verandah, one hand on the huge doorknob, and the white door moved inwards slightly at the pressure.

'Have all the cobwebs flown away?'

'What few there were, yes.'

'And you're not cold?'

She shook her head, unable to see his face clearly. There sounded to be a caress in his voice as he said softly, 'Sleep well. Goodnight, Irene.'

The words of the old song were in her mind as she went dreamily along to her own room.

During the next few days she was kept extremely busy. Mrs Marron apologised for the work which had accumulated since the departure of the last girl she had employed and except at mealtimes Irene saw little of the two cousins. They were both out all day, and Alex complained that he was very disappointed as only once had she been to look at the little penguin, who was steadily gaining strength and becoming utterly adorable, and when he did happen to be free Irene was busy in the study. His mother said sweetly that that was why she wanted a secretary, and it was not as though he was friendless and dependent upon the girl for company. On the contrary, she pointed out, Alex had not been in one evening since Irene had arrived, and at that remark he looked slightly embarrassed.

'Another new flame?' asked Carl, and the look flung in his direction was not one of cousinly affection.

The work was interesting and Irene found she was becoming intimately connected with the project in hand and delved back through earlier correspondence so she would have a better understanding about what she was doing. Her thoroughness met with Mrs Marron's wholehearted approval. On two occasions they drove to the gorge alone and the girl felt a rising indignation against the as yet unknown instigators of the idea to violate the place. She wanted to keep it as it was as fiercely as did the other woman, in its natural state, a peaceful reserve for locals and visitors alike. So she was willing to sit for hours and take dictation and Mrs Marron often retired early, satisfied that she could now get done all she wanted to do. Letters were written to many influential people and to the press, others had to be answered, and long articles were typed and later appeared in the newspapers.

When Carl read them he scowled. They were well written, precise and very much to the point. Aunt Kate certainly did not believe in pulling her punches. He knew quite well that some of the barbs were aimed at him personally, yet in the house the subject was never mentioned; she treated him as she had always done. It was as though there were two sides to her nature, the family one and the fanatical one, as there were two sides to his own nature.

He began the habit of wandering into the study later in the evening, when Irene was alone and working on the last of her notes. She would greet him with reserved warmth, nod towards one of the comfortable chairs and indicate that she would not be long. Usually within minutes of his arrival she would carefully sort out the typewritten pages, place some in a folder, others were put ready for Mrs Marron's signature and all were put neatly out of sight in a drawer. The typewriter was then covered and Irene would get to her feet. Carl wished he could reach over and lift some of the papers to comment upon her work; even from where he was sitting it looked neat and businesslike.

'Different from typing legal documents?' he asked one evening, and she nodded. 'They must have been very dry at times.'

'And revealing. Wills that were invidious, divorce actions that were cruel, other cases that were full of hatred and not—nice.'

'So you're happy here,' he stated.

'Very happy,' she smiled, and knelt down on the rug to stretch her hands out to the warmth of the fire. 'I haven't yet got over the thrill of leaning out of my window and picking an apple. I now eat one every morning while dressing. And it's you I must thank for being here,' she added shyly. 'You could have chosen one of the others——'

'They couldn't compare with you,' he muttered. 'In appearance or in their capability.'

86

'As I had no references you had no idea what my capabilities were,' she answered, lowering her head so he would not see the expression in her eyes, 'beyond my letter of application.'

Carl shook his head. 'I rang a friend of mine who knew your Mr Finlayson. He gave me a very glowing description of all you had done and could do. Apart from the business part of it all he also spoke in even more glowing terms about you personally. Mac Camden, you may remember him.' He was watching her closely and smiled at the way she lifted her head.

'Mac? So you knew him too! I knew him well, he took me to dinner once or twice——'

'He's married.'

'He wasn't then,' she cried with spirit. 'And Mr Finlayson was always with us. Usually it was to celebrate the successful end to one of the cases——'

'Oh, Irene!' he was laughing at her now. 'Did you really believe I thought you would go dining and wining with a married man?' He stood up and pulled her to her feet, looking down into her face in a way he had never looked at her before. 'I think I know you better than that. By the way, I'm going to ask Aunt Kate if she can do without you for the day on Sunday. I want to take you to Tarrentall. Will you come?'

Would she go? Her eyes were shining as she lifted her head, but her voice was low and controlled as she answered, 'Thank you, yes. I'd love to see it.'

CHAPTER 6

Aunt Kate was hesitant when Carl made his request at breakfast time the following day. She appeared to be giving the matter so much thought that it was Alex who broke the silence and became eloquent, accusing his cousin of enticing Irene away from Glendene.

'I'm not doing anything special on Sunday, so I should take her out,' he cried, and looked at the girl seated opposite to him as he added disparagingly, 'There's nothing so special about Tarrentall. It's a few acres larger than this place and from it you can see the Western Tiers. That's about all it can claim to either prosperity or beauty!'

'If Irene is to see more of Tasmania she couldn't do better than to start with a close view of the Western Tiers. She hasn't been anywhere yet.' Carl waited, but there was no contradiction to his remark, he thought wonderingly. Most girls would have cried 'Oh, but I have! I've been along the coast with your aunt and seen the most beautiful gorge——'

'I'll take you to the Great Lake, which is three thousand feet above sea level,' said Alex, 'and to get there you go *up* the Western Tiers, so you would have a much more intimate view of the mountains and the countryside below.'

'It's too far for a half day trip——'

'Not in my car it isn't. What kind of a heap do you drive?' asked Alex jeeringly.

'I meant to look at everything properly after spending all morning at Tarrentall and allowing for many stops in between,' exclaimed Carl patiently.

Irene glanced sideways at Mrs Marron, who was listening to this exchange of words with a faint smile on her lips.

'Isn't this all exciting?' she asked.

'Exciting?' Mrs Marron looked questioningly into the brown eyes, wishing it was her son who had made the request to take the girl out for the day.

'Yes. To have them almost fighting over me!'

There was a ripple of laughter round the table and even Netta, who had been standing near the dark oak sideboard, with a silver platter in one hand and some letters in the other, smiled slightly at the tone of Irene's voice and the mirth in her face, but the smile vanished as she looked at the others. The eyes of the two men were on the girl and Mrs Marron was sitting back in her chair, her face crinkled with amusement. With her back turned she quietly put down the platter and glanced at the letters, shuffling them in her hand as she moved towards the table.

'Your mail. Mr Elliott brought it out,' she said as she put them in front of Mrs Marron, and she managed to flick at the top envelope which slid across the table towards Carl. He could not help but see that it was an official one with 'On Her Majesty's

Service' in black letters across the top. He raised his eyes and his aunt looked at him as she reached for it, knowing as well as he did that this was the decision which would affect one or the other of them.

'I'll attend to these later,' she murmured, and put them beside her plate.

'None for me?' asked Alex.

'Not this morning.' Netta flounced out of the room.

'Your cheques must have all come yesterday,' said Irene comfortingly, wishing there had been one from Fran. Surely even on a honeymoon she could find time to send a picture postcard.

The wheelchair was moved from the table and Carl stood up. 'About Sunday, Aunt?'

'Yes, you may take Irene to Tarrentall for the day,' she agreed. She had a feeling of great optimism, that all had gone the way she wished, so let Carl take the girl through the lovely lanes to his home. By having her company he might forget some of his disappointment and the trip there would be some compensation for all the work Irene had done for her.

Her optimism was confirmed when she opened the letter. Denuded of all the officious jargon, it announced with pleasure the decision of the powers-that-be that the development scheme for the gorge was to be forbidden and that it was their intention to make the area a National Park so that it would always remain a place for recreation. Plans were also in hand to investigate another parcel of land which had been referred to on the day of the meeting at the gorge, with the idea of making that a nature reserve as well.

There was a deep sigh of satisfaction and when Irene came in the letter was handed over without comment, and the elder woman watched the expression change on the girl's face as she read the momentous news. They congratulated each other on their efforts, which, combined with others, had brought about this successful conclusion.

'And now more conservation?' asked Irene with a smile, putting the letter into a folder which contained the rest of the correspondence relating to the project.

'No, not at present. We'll rest on our laurels for a little while. There's no urgency about the other place referred to, as only one or two others, apart from us, know of the idea. I realise we can't stop the urban sprawl, but pressure must always be brought to bear when ideas such as that'—she nodded towards the folder Irene had out on the desk—'are brought forward, usually only for profit.'

'I've been so thankful to notice there are no high-rise buildings in the places we've visited.' Sitting in a chair facing Mrs Marron, Irene described her dislike of the offices she had visited, and the other woman's eyes had a glow in them as she listened. This was what she liked to hear!

'Have you other things in mind?' asked Irene with interest, returning to the original subject.

'Some short stories. The little penguin put an idea

into my head—it would be ideal for a children's book.' Mrs Marron moved across the room. 'Let's go and see it again. Alex will be there and he should be able to describe the habits of the little creature. I do like to get my facts straight!'

This was an idea which certainly pleased the girl as she walked beside the chair, down the ramp and on to the lawn. Brutus lifted his head, recognising the light footsteps, and stretched as he got to his feet and followed them from the house. Netta watched him gambol alongside Irene, saw her touch the smooth brown head, and she scowled.

Carl also watched them go to the kennels. He could hear his aunt's voice; it sounded carefree and happy, and he saw her wave to her son as he carried buckets from one enclosure to another, knowing from her attitude that the decision had gone the way she wanted and not the way he wished, and he turned from the window. From the study came the hum of a vacuum cleaner, then there was a sudden silence and he waited. When the noise did not resume he walked along the hall wondering if Netta had finished, fainted or fallen over—usually there was some clatter when she was cleaning. He and Alex had often teased her about the way she moved the furniture around and his aunt had wondered how the priceless pieces managed to survive without being scratched. The door was open and the room was empty, and Carl shrugged his shoulders. For once Netta had moved with speed and silence—perhaps she had suddenly remembered she had something cooking in the oven, for the cleaner was standing in the centre of the room. As he turned he glanced at the desk and then walked slowly towards it, for there was the same envelope which had fallen on to the dining table and beside it was the letter, as though it had been tossed down. He could not help but see it.

The fairy penguin was about nine inches high, and at the sound of approaching footsteps moved its little flippers in agitation and waddled awkwardly to Alex where it stood, its white chest puffed out, between his shoes. The wheelchair came to a standstill and in silence the others gazed in amazement and admiration at the engaging little creature, Irene's hand restraining Brutus from making a closer investigation.

'You will observe,' said Alex in the manner of a showman, 'the way it has rushed to me for protection. Usually it would stand between its mother's webbed feet, and as I'm the next best thing to a parent in its small mind, my shoes provide the comfort necessary to its peace of mind.' His voice changed and had a lilt in it. 'Isn't it really cute?'

'Keeping it alive must be one of your greatest achievements,' murmured his mother, and he nodded.

'I have reason to feel proud of myself. But it's been quite a job stuffing fish down its throat at regular intervals.'

'Would it be able to fend for itself if you returned

it to the sea?' asked Irene in a whisper, not wishing to disturb the enchanting picture the penguin made with its spotless white front and teal blue back. It was like a miniature gentleman in a dress suit.

'I very much doubt it.'

'So?' His mother looked at him with her head on one side.

'The best place for it would be the zoo,' he answered, and she nodded. 'But not yet. Martin must see more of it—hello, what have we coming down here?'

It was a large blue station waggon and in it were the owners of the shaggy dog, returned from holidays and coming to collect their pet. The dog recognised the sound of the car and began to whine and then to bark and Alex scooped up the penguin and put it out of sight, for from the car tumbled five boys, Irene guessed their ages from about three to twelve and they ran across the grass calling endearments to the dog, who was nearly hysterical with relief and excitement. As Alex let him out of his small enclosure Irene and Mrs Marron watched with smiles as the huge shaggy animal was hugged, squashed, kissed and petted. He bounded over to greet the parents, jumping up at them with joy, and then vanished under five bodies as they fell upon him to repeat their boisterous greetings.

'And Curly thrives on it!' commented the boys' mother with wonder. 'How are you, Mrs Marron?'

Conversation was general for a few minutes until the boys, still shouting, and the dog, still barking, clambered into the car. Alex watched them drive away.

'There's gratitude for you!' he grumbled. 'I spent hours holding his paw and giving him comfort as I tried to get it into his thick head that they would return, and I don't even get a backward glance by way of thanks!'

'Your reward was the looks on the children's faces,' murmured his mother, smiling at him, 'to find him safe and well. Wander round if you like, Irene, and look at everything. If I'm not mistaken Cinderella and her babies are over there. I want to know more about this penguin, Alex—hasn't it got a name?'

'Shoebox. Either gender.'

'And I thought you knew everything,' remarked Irene as she moved away, leaving mother and son laughing together. Alex stared after her.

'She even *looks* different from what she did when she arrived here,' he remarked wonderingly.

'I agree. How fortunate I've been this time, because she has settled down with the minimum of trouble and is the perfect secretary, for she enjoys her work.'

'So Carl knew what he was doing.'

'Definitely. There's so much he understands.' She wrinkled her nose. 'And so much he won't try to understand! I think he guessed at breakfast time that the plans he and his friends had in mind have all fallen through.' He looked pleased at this information, for although he said little about it Alex was one of his mother's strongest supporters in her efforts to keep the countryside in its natural state. 'Bring the shoebox out again, dear, I want to know all about the usual way of life of his kith and kin.'

The piglets did not look as interesting now they had grown and become rather grubby and Cinderella was too busy to lift her head as she rooted amongst the green stuff in the trough. Irene wandered further away, pausing now and then to speak to the inmates of the kennels and pens and reproving Brutus when he growled at some animal he took a dislike to, and she kept stopping to look round with pleasure. Beyond the fence was the orchard and with the labrador by her side she scrambled through and took her time selecting the apple she wanted, and, her choice made, she bit into the red skin and walked on idly. Tasmania had often been referred to as a little piece of England, and from here she could well believe it, having seen many books and calendars with pictures of the English countryside.

The land curved in an ever-changing panorama of rich farmland, with newly ploughed earth giving a contrast of red between the varying shades of greenness which were broken here and there by stands of trees, most bursting forth in all the glory of their autumn tints.

Five miles behind her was the sea, before her was the peak which had become a welcome and familiar sight from her bedroom window and behind that an imposing range of rocks which she now referred to with familiarity as the Western Tiers. And somewhere in between was Tarrentall which she was to visit with Carl on Sunday. Already she had an affection for the place, for the name itself intrigued her. Even Fran could not be as happy as she was at the moment.

Mrs Marron, her head full of information about the habits and behaviour of penguins, both large and small, had inspected the latest litter of puppies, stroked the nose of a foal and commiserated with a cat which had had the misfortune to lose a leg in an accident, and then looked round for her secretary. Alex pointed away to the right where Irene was sitting on the top bar of a gate, swinging her legs and obviously sharing another apple with Brutus, who was begging pathetically as though he had been starved for days.

'I'll leave her there,' she said softly. 'For there's nothing I need doing at the moment. Why don't you offer to take her out tonight, Alex? A change of scene and company would do her even more good.'

'Sorry,' he answered lightly. 'I have other plans.'

'And which of the village maidens is it this time, may I ask?' She looked at him shrewdly, for he appeared rather uncomfortable. For a moment he hesitated, wondering whether to tell her, and then decided to keep his own counsel. She would not be pleased.

'My secret,' he said smiling at her, a smile which took the sting out of the words, and she realised he had no intention of confiding in her. He was a man now and she could not insist on knowing where he was going and with whom; those days were long since past.

'I only hope she's nice,' she replied, and added to herself, 'As nice as Irene.'

He smiled again and was very thankful to notice that Irene had clambered down from the gate and was hurrying back through the orchard towards them.

'I'm sorry, have I kept you waiting?'

'Not at all. You could have stayed as long as you liked, and there's no need for you to return with me—make the most of the day, for the weather forecast isn't promising for the weekend.'

Swiftly she wheeled herself away and Alex watched her go with a frown between his eyes. He knew he had displeased her and Irene realised something had been said which had upset his mother, for the chair was moving more quickly than usual, as though its owner was angry. She decided that as she had been given the go-ahead to explore, and Brutus was with her, she would take him for a long walk, and after remarking that she would see him at lunchtime she set off briskly in the direction of the thicket. Alex shrugged his shoulders and returned to his work.

The weather did change, a cold wind blew in from Bass Strait and rain clouds built up over the distant hills. Leaves fell like a green and gold shower on the lawns, but Carl remarked that it might not last until Sunday, and even if it did they would be able to drive in comfort to Tarrentall and once inside the house the weather would not worry them.

His aunt watched him, thinking he did not seem unduly worried about the setback to the plans made by the construction company and which he must know about by now. Once or twice she heard him whistling to himself and occasionally in the evening he would be called to the phone, to return with an expression on his face she likened to Brutus enjoying what was left of the day's cream. And she wondered, for she knew her nephew almost as well as she knew her own son. Or thought she did, she added wryly to herself.

Irene busied herself in the study, emptying drawers and sorting out the contents, filing papers into different folders so they would be more accessible, and Mrs Marron assisted by having a spring-clean of the many magazines and papers which had piled up during the last months. During these days they grew to know each other, and a feeling of affection was there between them as Irene lost the last of her shyness and chattered away in a natural manner which warmed the other's heart. She found she was wishing Alex would take a much more serious liking to this child, but their companionship was not of that kind. It was more like that of brother and sister, for they teased each other and Alex said the most outrageous things which quite often brought equally outrageous answers, and mealtimes, when they were all together, were becoming hilarious and entertaining. Netta would listen, but she rarely smiled, a fact noted by all the others but not commented upon.

Friends often came in the evenings and Irene discovered Mrs Marron to be a bridge fiend. She herself was not keen on cards and was content to sit near the fire, curled up in one of the large comfortable chairs, reading through earlier stories and articles written by the woman in the wheelchair, occasionally lifting her head to watch the intent faces and listening to their remarks. It was all so much like home, 'Where folk do their own thing,' as Alex remarked when he came in late one night and cards were still being dealt.

'And I presume you've been doing yours?' asked his mother, and he grinned at her as he passed her chair.

'Decidedly!' He looked very satisfied with his lot as he sat down beside Irene.

Mrs Marron had noticed Carl watching the girl and wondered about this proposed visit to his own home. To the best of her knowledge he had only once offered to take anyone out there and the girl who had gone with him had shuddered in an affected way as she remarked upon its isolation. Less than a mile from the main road! Tarrentall would not look at its best after being shut up and empty for so long. Alex had been out once or twice and remarked that it smelt fusty and needed airing. Her sister appeared to be in no hurry to come back; her letters, which were read by all the family, were full of the places she had visited and the people she had met, including many references to a man she always called Sir Smith. She pondered about those things as Netta helped her prepare for bed, for the other woman was her friend and confidante and was rarely far away from her side.

'Carl goes into the study nearly every evening when she's there,' remarked Netta with a disapproving sniff, 'and sometimes they go out for a walk in the garden before the lass goes to bed.'

'Do they indeed!' Nothing had been mentioned about this. 'And what can they have in common? Irene isn't his type at all—the one he brought from Hobart was much more in his line; sophisticated and suave. One couldn't call my little secretary either of those things!'

Netta shrugged. It might have been easy to answer that question if Alex had been the one to spend the evenings with the girl from the mainland. Now he was the one who was always out and his cousin the one who stayed in.

'He'll be wanting something,' she muttered, and Mrs Marron frowned at her reflection as Netta brushed her white hair.

'That remark was quite uncalled-for,' she said severely, and received another shrug in reply.

When rain began to fall in earnest and the clouds lowered themselves to almost touch the tops of the high trees, it was decided not to waste time, and as ideas were so fresh in her active mind Mrs Marron sat before the fire with her eyes closed, speaking her thoughts aloud, and Irene, as her pencil raced along the lines, was taken back to her childhood when her mother had read of whimsical animals who could talk and get into scrapes and out of them as she and Fran and their brother had done. These stories were being created solely for children and were fantasy at its best. Naturally the penguin's name was Peter, and he was as lovable as the real one, who was now becoming increasingly curious about all that was going on around him. Or her, Irene added to herself, for Alex had informed her that only a penguin could tell the sex of another penguin.

When three stories were completed about Peter it was decided to drive to the coast, for the little creature had put other ideas into Mrs Marron's head and she said she would have the feel of her next character if they were watching the sea. As Irene settled in the car she remembered Carl warning her she might have to take dictation on a headland in a gale, and that was precisely what happened that day. Bass Strait was living up to its reputation of being one of the wildest stretches of water as winds and currents rushed between the island and the mainland two hundred and fifty miles away with all the forces of the oceans behind them. A howling wind drove the sea against the rocks in a fury of foam and spray and the spindrift covered the car, which was the only one foolhardy enough to venture on to the headland. Irene felt as though they had the world to themselves.

The new character was a seal. There was accuracy in the description of the waters in which it lived, humour in its behaviour and everything to please and interest a child in the story of its adventures and misadventures. Regretfully Irene closed the note-book when her employer ceased to speak.

'I'd almost begun to see Sylvester frolicking on the water's edge, waving his flippers at the children paddling nearby! I just don't know how you do it,' she said, and the words could hardly be heard above the roar of the wind and the sea.

'It's a gift the good God gave me,' was the answer. 'And so I can share it with others. I only hope they get as much enjoyment out of it as I do. I think we'd better go back—friends are dining with us tonight and tomorrow you go to Tarrentall.' She hesitated. 'Don't be disappointed when you see it, Irene. My sister has been away for many months and Carl only goes over there when he feels he ought to check that the place is still standing, which isn't often. He's too busy with other things.'

'What exactly is his job?' asked Irene as she started to turn the car.

Mrs Marron looked surprised. 'Don't you know? Hasn't he told you that he's very interested, along with half a dozen——' she instinctively ducked her head as a freak wave, driven to an even greater height by the wind, broke against the very top of the cliff and enveloped the car with water. Irene pressed her foot down hard on the accelerator and they shot forward, bumping over the rough ground, and as she was unable to see where they were going she missed a tree by inches. It was bent nearly double with the force of the gale and when she felt they were well away from any further danger she stopped and spun round in her seat, afraid the jolting had upset Mrs Marron.

'Are you all right?' she asked with concern.

'Yes, thanks to you.' And she stared in amazement, for exhilaration was the only word which could describe the look on the girl's face and in her eyes.

CHAPTER 7

BEYOND a few branches lying across the track and carpets of sodden brown and golden leaves on the lawns there was nothing else at Glendene to indicate the following morning that northern Tasmania had been stricken by a violent depression which had originated in the southern Indian Ocean. Sitting in silence in the sunlit dining-room at breakfast time, they listened to the early news which told of destruction along most of the coast, and the two women exchanged glances.

'We were fortunate to get away as we did,' said Mrs Marron quietly. 'And when we did.'

'Very!' retorted Alex. 'Of all the stupid things to do, to go to the headland in a gale! Didn't you realise it was something out of the ordinary? Both of you want your heads examining!'

'Irene enjoyed it,' murmured his mother as she indicated she wished the honey jar to be passed across the table.

The men looked at the girl. 'I did enjoy it,' she cried a trifle defiantly. 'And it didn't frighten me a quarter as much as gazing down from the seventeenth floor of one of those city buildings!'

'A child of nature,' remarked Alex.

'Then I hope you'll enjoy some of the sights we shall see this morning,' said Carl with amusement in his voice. 'The rivers will be foaming torrents after all the rain which fell on the mountains during the storm.'

'The falls would be well worth a visit,' commented his cousin, and smiled at the way Irene's face lit up at the thought of them. 'Why not go that way round, Carl, and let her see them?'

'I will,' he promised, and after that Irene could not get ready quickly enough.

It was wonderful to think she was going to spend the whole day in his company, to visit his home, the very name enthralled her, and to see what they had all told her would be fantastic sights along the way. Mrs Marron watched them leave immediately after breakfast and turned to find Netta by her side, hanging grimly on to the collar of her dog.

'Did he want to go too?' she asked, smiling, but the smile died away as she saw the look in the housekeeper's eyes. Alex, standing beside her, saw it too and he said, with emphasis and candour,

'If you're jealous of the way Brutus follows Irene around, beloved, you have only yourself to blame. You never take him out for walks——'

'How can I? I've enough to do looking after you,' snapped Netta, and spun round on her heels to go indoors, dragging Brutus with her.

Mother and son looked at each other. 'I hope she isn't going to make things unpleasant for Irene because of Brutus!' exclaimed Mrs Marron. 'I like the girl and we get along well together—she's the most natural little thing, and I don't want her to leave

Glendene.'

'And you can't tell Netta that because you can't do without her at Glendene either.' Alex had a shrewd idea that in the past Netta had been the cause of some of the hasty departures of the other girls, and he frowned, suddenly realising how his mother, his aunt, his cousin and himself were treated as though she owned the lot of them. Thinking back over the years he realised how Netta ruled the roost, and she had been more possessive towards him than his understanding mother had ever been. He wondered what she would have to say when he exploded his bombshell, as he had every intention of doing in the near future, but whatever Netta thought or said would mean nothing to him compared with how his mother would react to his news.

'No, I couldn't manage without her. She understands me and can help in ways no one else can, and that includes you, my son.' He nodded, knowing full well what she meant. On her bad days it was always Netta who was by her side; it was to her she turned when she was sick or afraid, for she knew what to do to ease the pain and make her comfortable; in a sickroom she was as good as any nurse. 'Are you going out today?'

He shook his head. 'I've plenty to do here, and Martin is coming to play with his penguin. There are others coming too, to look at some of the puppies.'

'It's time homes were found for them, for there seems to be a surprising number all of a sudden.'

'And have you noticed how quite a few resemble Brutus?' he asked, smiling at her cheerfully, and she laughed.

Totally unaware that she had been the cause of some unpleasantness at Glendene, Irene sat beside Carl as he drove slowly along the narrow roads which were bordered for the most part with hawthorn hedges, bright now with sprays of red berries. She caught glimpses of small lakes, swiftly running streams, and if she gave an exclamation as something caught her eye he obligingly came to a stop. To look at the sky it was difficult to imagine it as it had been the day before; now it was blue and the air was crystal clear and the numerous peaks of varying heights and contours popped up all over the place and made her cry out with delight. Carl knew the names of most, for despite his air of sophistication he loved his homeland and as a boy had explored all the surrounding country in company with his father.

As they continued leisurely on their way he regaled her with stories of Tasmania's early history, which had really started when Abel Tasman sailed down the east coast in 1642, the first recorded European to sight the island, and she listened with rapt attention. She was a flattering companion, for she rarely interrupted and was genuinely interested in all he had to say. Glancing at her out of the corner of his eyes, he thought she looked like a little bird; her brown hair was ruffled by the slight breeze which came through the half open window, the brown eyes were alert and as she occasionally looked at him they had that intriguing gleam of mischief which amused him. She wore a suit of nut-brown which was flecked with orange and cream and had an orange-coloured silk scarf round her throat.

He turned off the road near the Forth river and headed towards the falls, leaving the car when the track petered out into a narrow path which followed a foaming stream. Carl slipped his hand through her arm to assist her, for it was wet and slippery underfoot, and they slipped and slithered, laughing as each tried to hold up the other. Then before them were the falls, and with the roar of turbulent water nearly deafening her Irene gazed upwards with her head flung well back and with the spray falling on her cheeks, forgetting even her companion in the wonder of this moment. He could not make himself heard above the noise and held up seven fingers and waved his hand upwards to indicate that there were seven falls in all. Maidenhair fern grew in thick profusion in all the damp crevices, the delicate fronds drooping under the fine spray which filled the air, overhead tall trees filtered the sunlight and on fallen logs nearby pale green lichen covered the old bark.

'This must be paradise,' she murmured as she continued to stand there, lost in admiration of the wild beauty of the falling, foaming water.

Carl touched her arm and she turned towards him, wondering as she did so why she had ever thought him to look ruthless. Wearing a thick high-necked polo sweater and with his hair falling over his forehead, he looked relaxed and carefree; he was smiling down at her in a way he had done once before in the study at Glendene and a delicate flush covered her cheeks. Regretfully she moved away as he turned back along the path.

'I don't think there's any need for me to ask if you enjoyed that,' he remarked as soon as they were far enough away from the falls to make conversation possible, and she shook her head, still listening to the roar which was gradually being dulled by the trees and the distance. As she opened the car door she asked hopefully,

'And are there more around and about?'

'Yes, but if we're to reach Tarrentall before lunch we haven't time to see them. There'll be plenty of opportunities in the months ahead to visit all the beauty spots; I can guarantee hundreds of them.'

'You sound confident I shall still be here.'

'Aunt Kate is very satisfied, so why shouldn't you be around in the spring? You like the work, don't you?'

'I'm thoroughly enjoying it. Your aunt is a very gifted person and it's really a privilege to work with her. She has a wonderful imaginative mind and so many varied interests.'

'You mean such as conservation?' he asked idly, and she nodded, still busy looking at the countryside as the car rounded bends and crossed narrow bridges. 'You agree with all her views on that subject?'

'Of course I do! Who wants to spoil land such as

this——' for a moment she hesitated. She knew it was common knowledge that Mrs Marron was one of the leaders in the fight to preserve beauty spots such as the one they had just visited, so it was all right to discuss the subject with her nephew, but not for one moment did she consider confiding in him of any plans for the future, 'with projects as have been suggested in various parts of Tasmania and other places? Don't you agree with all she and her friends are doing?'

'Not altogether. Everything can't be kept as it was in the past. These days, with an ever-increasing population, one must move with the times and supply what's necessary for the wellbeing of the people.'

'Oh yes! But so much must be left in its natural state for them to enjoy,' she argued. 'Everyone needs solitude at times, what better place to find it than on a river bank or a mountainside which is as it was before humans ever came to this part of the world?'

'You're nearly as fanatical as Aunt Kate! There are two sides to every question, and I don't see that the countryside would be ruined because a few more homes were being built on virgin ground.'

Irene gave an impatient shrug of her shoulders. 'Not only homes. Factories, mills, mines if there happens to be a mineral of use underfoot. Really, you sound as though you have a vested interest in some of these schemes!'

'I have,' he admitted, and she spun round in her seat to stare at him. 'Has no one told you? Didn't

Aunt Kate tell you that though I'm an architect by profession I also have a great interest in developments.'

'Oh, Carl!' her eyes widened in disbelief. 'No, I wasn't told. I can't believe it of you!' She made it sound as if he had committed a misdemeanour.

'And have I gone down in your estimation because of it?' he asked plaintively.

Irene did not answer; she turned to look at the wide Forth river as they crossed it again and there was a slight frown beween her eyes. More than once she had sensed a feeling of aggression between aunt and nephew, and now she knew the reason for it. Thankfully she realised she had done or said nothing which could have revealed any of Mrs Marron's hopes and plans for the future, but she was conscious of a deep sense of disappointment that Carl was one of her adversaries in her fight for conservation.

'Look over there,' murmured Carl, and obediently she turned her head. The land opened out into a beautiful setting with Mount Roland standing like a rocky sentinel near the picturesque town of Sheffield where in nearly every garden were heavily laden apple trees and huge piles of sawn timber ready for the fires which would be needed during the severity of the coming winter. Irene became too engrossed in trying to look at everything all at once to talk to him, and Carl smiled to himself as he left the tarred road and followed a gravel track, similar to the one leading to Glendene, and on the top of a rise he stopped and waved towards the valley which opened out below them.

There was another river, small in comparison to the others they had crossed; it looped and turned through pastures so thick and green that the cattle could hardly be seen. Its banks were lined with tall poplars, some bare as a result of the previous day's buffeting, others which had been sheltered from the winds were still dignified and beautiful in their covering of gold. There were more hawthorn hedges, and in the midst of it all, surrounded by trees, was a large house and behind it, stark against the blue sky, the Western Tiers rose three thousand feet above the countryside.

'Tarrentall,' murmured Carl.

It had been built of grey stone and ivy clung to it in parts, a rambling place with no architectural design; its beauty was in the way it blended and became as natural as the trees and the landscape. Chimneys thrust themselves up high above the slate roof; it looked solid and comfortable and Irene fell completely in love with it the moment her eyes rested upon it. She thought of Mrs Morgan, gallivanting round beauty spots on the other side of the world, and of Carl living at Glendene, leaving this house to brood alone over the memories of yester-years when so many Morgans had lived, loved and died within its protective walls. Her imagination was becoming too vivid, she thought, as she continued to gaze at the vista below her; other things were conjured up in her mind and she burst out,

'How would you like all that to be subdivided for development? To have those old trees cut down and burnt out, to have that lovely countryside dug with machinery for sewage and water pipes?' Her voice rose with indignation. 'Then to have the view destroyed from the house, if that wasn't pulled down as well, by brightly coloured rooftops, with chimneys and TV antennae stuck up all over the place!'

'You certainly are a good mate for Aunt Kate!' There was a slight edge to his voice. He had hoped for and expected sighs of delight, an indrawn breath at the beauty of the setting of his home; it was one reason he had wanted her to see it.

'I happen to be a country girl myself,' she answered shortly, and Carl surveyed her in amazement.

This was a different girl from the one he had known at Glendene. Her voice rang out clearly and defiantly and there was a fiery glint in her eyes; she was looking at him with an expression that suggested that he had already done the things she had mentioned.

They moved swiftly down past the poplars and along the weed-covered track to the large gates which were open and cattle grazed amidst the shrubs on either side. Large beds which were covered with weeds still had odd roses flowering on long straggly branches, and Irene immediately visualised daffodils in profusion flaunting their colour beneath neatly pruned bushes in the spring. All around there were trees, elms and oaks, grown to a great height, with an odd jacaránda or flowering peach here and there.

'It has plenty of trees,' he remarked, and looked at her hopefully. Irene smiled.

'It wouldn't be the same at all without them.'

The car drew up at the few steps which led to the wide crazy paved portico which was covered with leaves, empty cigarette packets and definite evidence that the cattle had been in possession up here too.

'What a mess!' muttered Carl as he stood on the top step.

'How long is it since you were last here?'

'Oh, months ago. I haven't had the time——'

She gave him a look almost of scorn as he walked to the front door. If he had bothered with his own home and left the building of other places, she thought rather viciously, it would not be in this state now. The front door opened slowly, the hall was wide with doors opening from it on either side and there was a musty smell about everything. Apologetically he looked at her.

'I'm sorry. I was going to show you my home as I remembered it. Not this dead and dusty place——' his voice faded into silence as they wandered from one room to another, pulling back the heavy curtains to let in the sunshine. The furniture was covered with dust sheets, and unthinkingly Irene whipped some off and looked keenly at what was underneath.

'No sign of damp,' she said with relief in her voice.

'Oh, the house is solid, I can guarantee that. But it smells!'

'Let's open the windows and let in some fresh air.'

There were two large rooms at the front of the house which she presumed had been used for entertaining, a dining-room and a breakfast-room and all had large fireplaces and she could see them filled with large glowing logs. Four bedrooms had two bathrooms between them and which were modern, as was the kitchen, but after the one at Glendene, with its warmth and smell of cooking and the boxes of kittens or puppies on the rug near the fire, this looked bare and not at all inviting. Back in the hall they looked at each other.

'Well?' asked Carl.

'It's a wonderful house, spoilt,' Irene answered frankly. 'Surely it meant more to you than this! To let it get into such a state because you were busy.'

'So what do *you* suggest I do with it?'

'Live in it. Bring your friends here, make it come to life again.'

He half turned from her. 'That might be possible if my mother returned home. But she was always the social butterfly and the London scene will appeal to her more than this now my father is gone. Aunt Kate has an inborn love of the land—what a contrast in sisters!'

'A housekeeper? Couldn't you get someone to——'

'Do you honestly think a housekeeper would be the one to make it feel like home?' he asked roughly.

'Even Netta, who has been at Glendene since she was in her teens, wouldn't have the touch necessary to make Tarrentall as it was. She cooks and cleans and looks after Aunt Kate, she doesn't make the house feel alive as a family would. It needs someone who loves it.'

'I'm sorry.' Moving to his side, she gently touched his arm and changed the subject. 'We brought lunch, so let's eat it in here. Then you can show me round outside and let me see the cattle and the horses—I noticed one or two in the paddocks. I want to look at those rocky peaks too. Don't spoil my day by being upset because the house isn't as it should be,' she was smiling at him. 'So far it's all been wonderful.'

'Even to my confession that I'm against most of what Aunt Kate is fighting for?'

'Maybe you'll change your mind.'

'What are you trying to do? Reform me?'

'I think it would be a waste of time to try.'

'And what gives you that impression?'

'Your stubbornness,' she answered, and he laughed.

'You've changed since the day I met you at the motel,' he remarked as they walked to the front door and stood in the autumn sunshine. 'Then you were a timid little sparrow, now you're a——'

'Bird of Paradise?' she asked hopefully.

'I was going to compare you with an eagle, poised to strike, with all claws bared.' Her laughter echoed back along the hall. 'Bird of Paradise indeed!' he scoffed, and grabbed hold of her hand. 'Come on, let's find the lunch basket.'

Later Carl was amazed at her knowledge as they explored the grounds of the house. She lamented over the overgrown flower beds, even pulling out a few weeds from around some shrubs which she named with accuracy. She did not draw back when they went into the fields and the cattle raised their heads to survey them with placid eyes or when a horse came towards them, proudly tossing his head.

'It looks like the one I used to ride at home,' murmured Irene, looking at it with appreciation and thinking it would be hard to handle after running free for so long.

Carl glanced at her slim figure and at the animal which had halted a few yards from them. 'Surely not! You'd never be able to hold him.'

'I may be small, but I'm certainly not helpless,' she retorted. 'The three of us were taught at a very early age how to ride and my brother once dared me to try one we'd been forbidden to touch.' A smile crossed her face. 'We both did so, but I stayed on longer than he did! After that I rode the horse regularly, we became quite friendly.'

He was certainly learning a great deal about this young lady, mused Carl as an inquisitive calf confronted her and she rubbed its nose, remarking on its condition. It was a fat and placid Jersey heifer.

'Ours at home were all beef cattle,' she said. 'Where do you send the milk from here?'

He hesitated. 'I think Alex has it collected for

the cheese factory.'

'But you aren't sure?'

'As long as I get my cheque each month I can't say I'm worried as to where the milk goes.'

'What a mercenary attitude he has,' she remarked to the calf who was padding along beside her, and Carl realised that the colour in her cheeks was of anger. Anger that he took so little interest in his home and the land around it, which proved she liked it despite its air of dilapidation.

Only one man was in the milking shed and he was surprised and pleased when they walked in. Irene was introduced and stood on one side as Mick went into details of all that was happening at Tarrentall in the absence of the owner, and she thought how fortunate he was in having men who could be trusted, then realised it was Alex who was responsible for the smooth running of the place.

'It's a long time since you were last here,' remarked Mick. 'And your mum, when is she coming home?'

'I have no idea when she'll be back.' There was a shrug of the broad shoulders.

'So the house is to stay shut up?'

Carl nodded and moved further along to look at the stalls where the cows were milked; they would soon start congregating together at the gate nearby and would follow, one behind the other, to take their turn in the milking shed. Mick glanced at the girl, wondering at the relationship between her and the boss, for he rarely brought anyone out here, and

Irene, meeting his eyes, guessed what was passing through his mind and turning abruptly, went outside to gaze at the rocky crags in the distance.

She knew with great certainty that she wanted Carl to return home and take over the running of the place from his cousin and that she wanted him to bring her with him to live in this old grey house. The discovery of her love for him was not altogether a surprise. There had been something there, in her heart, since the day she had first met him, when he had stood beside her, smiling as he announced she could go to Tasmania. Then she had thought it gratitude, now she knew differently.

CHAPTER 8

WHEN Carl followed her outside he announced that they would shut up the house and leave, for he had thought of showing her something else which would give her pleasure, but it would mean a long drive and they would not reach Glendene until late. A phone call from the nearest town would put his aunt's mind at rest, and without comment Irene walked down to the car, leaving him to return to the house and lock the door. She watched as he went up the wide steps, thinking that the curtains had not been drawn back over the windows but the weak sunshine would not damage the carpets or the furniture and would perhaps warm the place a little. Her heart ached for the loneliness of the house; it looked forlorn, and as she heard the slam of the front door she winced.

Carl turned and thought her expression was one almost of wistfulness, and as they drove away in a different direction, heading towards Deloraine, she was very quiet and more than once he glanced down at her by his side. On the outskirts of the town he stopped at the post office to ring Glendene.

'Netta answered,' he remarked as he slid in behind the wheel. 'She sounded quite put out about something and said it would make no difference what time we got back as things would still be the same!'

'Your aunt?' She turned towards him swiftly.

'If there'd been anything wrong with her she would have told me immediately,' he answered complacently. 'You'll like Deloraine, it's one of the richest farming areas on the island.'

'And what's that in the distance?' She leaned forward to peer through the screen.

'Quamby Bluff, another peak such as you can see from your bedroom window. Oh, there are so many things to be seen around here, apart from the rest of Tasmania. This is the Meander River—oh, boy, just look at it!'

'It's certainly not meandering today,' she said in an awed voice. Swollen from the previous day's storm, it was a raging torrent and groups of sightseers lined the banks to watch. 'Is this what you wanted me to see?'

Carl shook his head. 'No, where I'm taking you will be even more impressive.'

Settling back again in her seat, she thought, 'Ask me to go with you and I'll go, without fear or question, to the ends of the earth.'

Less than an hour later they reached the outskirts of Launceston, the second largest city on the island, and its many parks and gardens were ablaze with autumn colour. Irene remarked that she had never seen such variety in scenery in one day. Only minutes away from the centre of the city Carl turned into a car park and muttered something rude under his breath at the number of cars parked there. It was only because a family sedan drew out of line on its way out that he was able to find a space at all. In silence she walked beside him, wondering what he was going to show her and thinking it must be something out of the ordinary if all the other car owners were looking at it too.

It was more than out of the ordinary. It was an awe-inspiring spectacle of raging torrents of water rushing through the Cataract Gorge, where the South Esk River had carved its way through rocky hills during centuries of time, and crashing up against the rocks and up the rocky cliffs. It was a sight never to be forgotten and the thunder of the water made conversation totally impossible, a wild and untamable example of Nature's combined beauty and terror.

'Over there,' Carl bent his head until it touched hers and shouted in her ear, pointing to one side of the gorge, 'is a footpath constructed along the walls of the cliffs and when the river is running normally it's possible to walk to what's called the First Basin.'

'I'd hate to try it now!' she shouted back, thinking that within a minute the force of the flow would dash a human body to pieces against the cliff side.

'There are lawns and gardens and glorious trees up there, also peacocks——'

'It's a wonder you don't want to develop that,' she murmured, and was thankful he could not hear her.

They lingered for a long time, until the shadows lengthened and the sun went down behind the trees

123

at the top of the high cliffs. Her eyes were shining as he finally led her away and when at last he could speak normally he just said, 'Well?'

'I doubt if I'll ever forget such a wonderful sight! I suppose we were fortunate in seeing it, because of the storm yesterday?'

He nodded as he unlocked the car. 'It isn't often it happens. Today was exceptional, it must have pulled out all the stops because you were here. Now we'll have a meal at one of the motels and then dawdle home.'

'Your aunt may be wondering where we are.'

'I did tell Netta we would be late,' he said reproachfully. 'Surely we're old enough to stay out after dark?'

Irene chuckled, he sounded so much like Alex, and over an hour later, settled back to enjoy the eighty-mile drive, her only regret being that she could see nothing beyond the beam of the headlights. In the glimmer from the dashboard light she watched the strong hands on the wheel, and occasionally, as though she was glancing at the road on his side, she could see his face. He still looked relaxed and carefree. Once or twice as they took a corner at speed their shoulders touched and her whole body responded with a glow of warmth which surprised her and made her wonder how she would react if his arms ever held her tightly to him.

She was thankful when he began to describe the spectacular new bridge which had been built across the Tamar River thirty miles from Launceston nearer the sea, enabling motorists to tour both sides of the lovely river, although, she thought disconsolately, it proved his thoughts were on a wonder of engineering and not herself.

As they sped down the gravel track towards Glendene Carl frowned and she leaned forward in her seat. There were no lights, usually the one outside glowed in welcome and others shone through uncurtained windows. One or two howls, followed by barks, came from the direction of the kennels, and Irene turned.

'Alex? Surely he's here?' The animals always seemed to sense his presence and they were quiet. Now even Brutus barked as the car drew up at the gate. 'Something must have happened.'

She felt guilty as she hurried up the path, for the house was strangely silent. The barks changed to a whine of welcome as the big labrador recognised her footsteps and as she opened the door he jumped up and absently she fondled his ears. Netta was standing in the kitchen doorway, a tired strained look on her plump face, and the look in her eyes darkened to something else as she watched her dog.

'So you've come at last, have you?'

'Where is everyone? Is something wrong?' Carl stopped beside Irene and stared at the housekeeper.

'You may well ask! Your aunt has gone to bed and your cousin is in disgrace!' burst out Netta, and Carl's eyebrows drew together. 'But it's not my place to tell you all about it. And if you're going into her room mind you don't upset her any more. She's had enough this day, I can tell you, with shocks like that. You should have been with her.' The look she gave Irene was full of venom as though she blamed her for whatever had happened while she was gallivanting round the countryside.

'Why didn't you say something was wrong when I rang?' asked Carl.

Netta sniffed and disdained to answer, so the other two hurried along the hall to Mrs Marron's bedroom and Carl tapped gently on the door.

'Aunt! May we please come in?'

There was a murmur which he took as one of assent. It was a beautiful room, high-ceilinged as were the rest, with a thick carpet on the floor, long curtains in a soft gold across the windows and at one end a wide bed covered with a matching spread. Mrs Marron was propped up against the pillows; her eyes were wide and dark against the pallor of her face, and her nephew hurried across to her side and slipped his arm round her shoulders.

'You're ill! Why wasn't the doctor sent for?'

'He couldn't help me,' she muttered, resting her head against him for a moment.

'But if you've had a shock—Netta said something —what's the matter?' He no longer looked relaxed, there was anxiety in his eyes and his whole demeanour as he bent over her.

'Your mother——'

'No!' He moved back to stare at her and she lifted her hand to touch his face.

'No, not that, not what you're thinking.' Suddenly

she sat up higher against her pillows and her voice became shrill. 'She rang from London not long after you left here this morning. It was a great pity you were unable to take the call.'

'Well?' snapped Carl impatiently. 'What had she to say? Is she coming home?'

'No, she is not. She wanted us to know that she was married and that now she's Lady Smith——'

He stared down at her unbelievingly. 'Married?'

'That's what I said,' cried his aunt. 'Lady Smith. Oh, she'd mentioned this man, hadn't we all laughed about Sir Smith? Well, he's now her husband, your stepfather, Carl, and your mother is to live in an ancient castle or some such. I was too stunned to take everything in.'

'Oh, why didn't you tell her to ring Tarrentall?'

'Because you had the phone disconnected!'

'Married!' He pushed his hand through his hair and Irene's heart ached for him as she realised how the news had shocked and surprised him. 'That means she won't be returning, that Tarrentall will stay empty.'

'It's been empty for months, years, and well you know it. She's written to you and said she would ring again later.' There was a quiver in her voice and Carl wondered why his mother's marriage had upset her to this extent, then remembered that Netta had used the plural when speaking of shocks.

'There's something else?' he asked more gently, and she nodded. Her fingers plucking at the sheets and Irene moved to the other side of the bed, put-

127

ting her hand sympathetically on the thin one nearest to her, and was astonished at the strength in it as it turned to grasp hers.

'Yes, there is something else. To take my mind off what I'd just heard I went down to the kennels. Martin came to play with his penguin and Alex had said others were coming to look at the puppies. I stayed there watching the antics of all the young things when another car arrived.' Her voice broke and Irene's fingers tightened round the hand in hers. 'It was Renate with the twins.' She stopped and swallowed hard as though she was unable to get more words out.

'What was wrong with that?' asked Carl. 'They're adorable little minxes!'

'Oh, yes. But their mother—I couldn't help but see and I didn't want to understand, though it was so obvious in the way they looked at each other. Later I asked Alex to tell me if I was right. He admitted that it was true, they want to get married.'

'Renate?'

Irene, not knowing the girl to whom they referred, waited in silence, suddenly remembering the look which had crossed Alex's face the first time she had called in at the surgery in town and referred to herself in fun as the one love of his life. She had seen the strain then and had seen it since, despite his apparent lightheartedness.

'She's rather a sweet little thing,' remarked Carl, 'and has been very unlucky since leaving Australia and coming to live here. She didn't ask for help from anyone when she lost her husband, she battled on alone, and everyone has admired her for it.'

'She's a widow with twin sons, and if she marries Alex she'll come to live here. Glendene must only belong to a Marron. It's belonged to them for generations.' She was becoming even more agitated, and Irene lifted her head and looked at Carl.

'Of course Glendene will belong to a Marron,' he answered soothingly. 'Alex is one, and he'll surely have a son of his own.'

'But if he doesn't her son, foreign born, will inherit the place!'

'Aunt, you aren't being your usual sensible self at all. At present such a possibility doesn't enter into the scheme of things.'

'Did you know he was meeting her?' she demanded to know. 'Have you been keeping this from me too?'

Carl shook his head. 'I had no idea who he was taking out or going to see. Alex knows so many girls —I guarantee he's taken out every one in the district. He's popular because he's such good company and has a way with both children and animals which endears him to everyone he meets. If they love each other and would be happy together surely it isn't such a bad thing? You must have known it would happen some day.'

'But not to a woman who's older than he is and who has been married before.' She turned from him with an impatient movement and buried her head in the pillows, her shoulders shaking.

Carl looked at Irene. 'Tell Netta to phone the doctor,' he whispered. 'She must have a sedative.'

This wild crying would bring on another of those dreadful headaches, and the more she brooded over what had happened the longer they would last and the worse they would become.

The doctor, a personal friend, promised to drive out immediately and Irene went into the lounge and sat before the fire, thinking of two sisters, obviously so different in temperament, one in England, happy in her second marriage, the other in Tasmania, unhappy because of her only son's proposed marriage. A cold nose thrust itself into her hand and Brutus offered his silent sympathy as he gazed up into her face. He knew something was wrong, for he had been severely reprimanded for barking, and Lulu, his constant companion in the house, was in her basket, whining softly to herself. Sitting together, they heard the doctor's car, heard the murmur of voices in the hall and then Carl came into the room and looked at them in the firelight. His hand which had reached for the switch fell to his side and he flopped down into the chair on the other side of the fireplace.

'I can't do any more,' he said quietly. 'Netta will stay with her.'

'Has Alex come home?'

'Not yet. He'll be very upset when he hears what's happened,' he said broodingly, and wished he was at Tarrentall, away from all this. It was the first time in many months, he thought wonderingly, that he had wanted to be in his own home.

'You know Renate? What's she like?' she asked curiously.

'Small. Rather like you in build, with long fair hair, plaited and twisted like a crown round her head.' He was gazing into the flames. 'She speaks good English with a faint accent and is well liked in the town. Her husband was a truck driver, the only job he could get when he arrived out here. He was killed in a smash near Burnie one night when his sons were about three months old.'

'And how old are they now?'

He wrinkled his brow in thought. 'Nearly four, I would think. Identical twins, little things who would appeal to Alex, and like all other little things they would respond to his friendliness.' He stood up abruptly and leaned against the wide mantelpiece staring down into the dancing flames. 'I don't know why Aunt is so upset about this. If Alex hasn't told her it was perhaps because he hadn't got round to popping the question, I very much doubt that it was because he was afraid to tell his mother. That sounds like his car now.'

'Go and meet him,' urged Irene quietly. 'You explain what's happened, don't let Netta get in first.'

'Why do you say that?'

She hesitated for a moment. 'I think she would immediately blame him and accuse him of being deceitful, shutting his mother out of his life. She's very possessive where your aunt is concerned.'

'So you've found that out too,' he said to himself

as he left the room.

Alex did not see his mother that night. Netta refused point blank to let him into the bedroom and as Mrs Marron was under sedation she would not have known he was there anyway. So he went into the lounge with Carl; Irene brought in a tray from the kitchen and still sitting in the firelight handed round cups of tea. Alex stared down at his shoes and there was no laughter in his voice as he told them quietly and frankly of his growing affection for the little Australian girl and her children and of the way she had gradually responded, finally admitting, only a few weeks ago, that she thought of him as he so obviously thought of her.

'Mother knew them as she knows nearly everyone in the district, and she greeted the three of them when they arrived in the friendly way she has, commenting on the way the boys were growing and laughing because she didn't know which was which. I wanted her to become accustomed to seeing more of them before telling her about my good fortune. I didn't realise Renate and I behaved any differently from—from what Irene and I would have done if we'd been playing with kids and pups!' He put in two more teaspoons of sugar in his cup and Irene did not comment that he had already put in four. 'We were just as usual, or so I thought. Evidently when you're in love you don't act or sound the same as you normally do.'

Irene broke a biscuit and concentrated her attention on making Brutus sit up for it. If what Alex said was true she would have to be very careful, but perhaps his remark only applied when two people realised their affection for each other was deep and true.

'Mother was too quick for me. Renate's car was not out of sight before she demanded an explanation of my intentions. It sounded so old-fashioned!' A very slight smile crossed his tired face. 'Especially when I assured her that they were quite honourable. But how *did* she know?'

'A woman's intuition,' murmured his cousin.

'I'm twenty-five and old enough to get married— surely she realised it would happen some time! She's never been possessive in that way, why then is she so upset?'

'I gathered the principal objection was because Glendene has always belonged to a Marron, and Aunt doesn't want another man's son to inherit it.'

'At least I should be given the chance of finding out whether I can have a son of my own before that argument arises!'

'By tomorrow your mother may see things in a different light,' murmured Irene comfortingly, speaking for the first time. She had been watching the varying expressions on the two faces. 'It was a shock and a surprise, but I'm sure when she has thought it over, and as she knows Renate, she'll think differently.'

'I sincerely hope you're right. for come what may I'm going to marry that girl.' He stood up and stretched. 'Have you enjoyed your day?'

'Very much,' Carl answered for them both. 'We went to the falls and after we left Tarrentall I took Irene to see the Gorge at Launceston. It was in full flood, I've never seen it like that before; it was awesome and rather frightening. Tarrentall,' he turned and stared down into the fire, 'looked empty and forlorn and it will evidently stay that way, for my mother is not coming back here. She phoned the news shortly after we left this morning that she is now Lady Smith, having married her aristocratic escort in London.'

'Good God!' His cousin stared at him in surprise. 'There's been no mention of an engagement—what a surprise! I suppose that will have upset Mum too. Why didn't she tell me when she came down to the kennels? She must have known then.'

Carl nodded. 'Yes, that was the first shock she received. But as Mother has been away for months I doubt if it will make much difference to Aunt Kate. They were never very close as their way of life and their interests were so very different.'

'But it will make a difference to you?' asked Alex shrewdly.

'Naturally. I would have liked to have seen her after all this time. And I would like to go back home again. But now Tarrentall will have to stay as it is.'

Vacant and cold, thought Irene as she went into the kitchen with the tray. Not even the winter sunlight which would stream through the uncovered windows would give those lovely rooms an air of occupancy. Tarrentall needed life and laughter, it needed constant attention to turn it into the home it had been years ago when Carl was young, before his father died. She blinked her eyes, and Brutus, who had followed her, hopefully eyeing the biscuit tin, was agreeably surprised as she knelt beside him and hugged his huge body in her arms.

CHAPTER 9

MRS MARRON stayed in her room for the next three days. Irene did not see her, as Netta was in her element keeping guard and the only person she allowed in, apart from the doctor, was Alex. What was said between mother and son the others never knew. Occasionally he would come out with his lips set in a thin line and a heavy frown between his eyes, then he would leave the house and drive into town. They all knew he was busy with his work, but they rarely saw him in the evenings and guessed he was spending his spare time with Renate and her sons.

Carl never went out in the evening; he seemed quite content to stay with Irene and the dogs in front of the roaring log fire, reading or idly discussing commonplace events. Occasionally he would entertain her with descriptions of Tasmania's early history, spreading maps out to show her where these events had taken place. Numerous phone calls came for him, including one from his mother, who was now on the Continent on her honeymoon.

'Well, she seems happy enough,' he remarked when he returned to the lounge after this conversation. 'And her husband sounds to have a very pleasant voice.'

'Oh, you spoke to him as well?' Irene looked very

interested.

'He hoped I would forgive him for rushing her into marriage, but he didn't want to let her slip through his fingers, as he's never met such a delightful scatterbrain in all his life.' He laughed down at her. 'We've all called Mother some things, but no one else to my knowledge has openly acknowledged her to be a delightful scatterbrain. I wish I could go in and tell Aunt Kate!'

'Is she really one?' she smiled as she gazed up into his face, wondering about this mother of his. Was she tall, or had her husband, Carl's father, passed on his height to his son?

'Oh, yes, and an inveterate chatterbox! Aunt has the family's brains, Mother was given the beauty, along with a vague docility which my father and I always found attractive. I think she used it to her advantage and Dad played along with her. After his death she couldn't stay in one place for any length of time. Even Tarrentall, which she loved, could not hold her interst. Without him it was merely a shell.'

Irene knew what he meant. If ever the impossible happened Tarrentall would only be home if Carl was with her to share it. She had thought a great deal about the place during the last few days, for there was little she could do in the study; all the short stories about the penguin and the seal had been typed and put on one side for alteration or correction when Mrs Marron was well enough, and for the rest of her time she had been out of doors, principally in the kennels where she assisted with the animals. She never asked questions of Alex and he was grateful for her reticence, accepting her offer of help with gratitude. Often she would have liked to have gone into the kitchen and sat at the large table to talk to Netta, but the housekeeper's attitude was one of aloofness and always she was within call of the invalid.

'If Aunt is still out of action tomorrow and doesn't want you to do anything for her would you like to go with me to visit Stanley?' asked Carl one evening.

'Stanley who?'

'A place called Stanley,' he explained with a smile. 'A small but well constructed port which, in poetic language, nestles beneath the beetling cliffs of the Nut. And that, my child, is a landmark which can be seen for miles, because it dominates the coastline.'

'It sounds interesting,' she said casually, glancing at him over the pages of a magazine. 'Are you planning a development site out there?'

'No, I am not!' He stared at her with anger in his eyes. 'I'm going on business. As I've already explained, I'm an architect and my services have been requested for the planning of two new homes. Therefore I want to visit the land on which they're to be built.'

'Thank you, in that case I'll be delighted to accept your invitation.'

He stood up, went out of the room and slammed the door. She had looked like a mischievous Willie Wagtail, but her remarks were beginning to get under his skin; evidently she intended to keep the flag flying while his aunt was indisposed.

The request to go with Carl was made formally and correctly through Netta, who stood like a sentinel by the bedroom door. The answer came in the affirmative.

'Please thank Mrs Marron from me. And I do hope she's very much better.' Irene wished she could sit beside her employer; if she could discuss penguins and seals surely it would be better for her than to lie there thinking about Alex?

'She's improving. Oh, and she hopes you have a nice day.' This was said because Netta had been given the message and knew the other would be listening.

Carl drove through the back roads to the town of Burnie and from the steep green slopes of the encircling hills they looked down on the township itself, the huge paper mills which he promised to take her round one day, Emu Bay and the port where at one of the wharves the Sydney–Tasmania ferry had just berthed. What amused and interested Irene was the way the railway line ran along past the piers and industrial area to the beach and then swung almost to the edge of a headland, skirting the outside of a sports oval, as though fearful of encroaching on the football and cricket pitches before resuming its way along the coast.

With her hair blowing in the breeze off the sea she looked the picture of delighted animation, and to him it was a novel and fascinating experience to have his attention drawn to something which had always been there and which he had not noticed before. He thought her more like a bird than ever, for she was never still; first she leaned to one side and then the other, turning her head to stare back at something and then spinning round to peer again through the windscreen.

Irene was supremely happy. Sitting beside the man she now knew she loved with all her heart, she had his whole attention, for this day, and even the weather was in keeping with her mood. It was clear but cold, everything stood out with great vividness, the rugged headlands and golden beaches, brilliant green fields and swiftly running streams—and then her voice died away in wonder as Carl made a deviation down a steep track to Boat Harbour where the sands were white and the sea so clear that shells and tiny fish could plainly be seen and the gulls were so friendly they perched on the bonnet of the car and peered at them through the windscreen.

There was something new to see at Port Latta, where Carl explained that a fifty-three-mile pipeline terminated here. Through it crushed ore was pumped from the mine site at Savage River and was bulk-loaded for shipment overseas. From there it was possible to see the Nut across the wide Sawyer Bay at Stanley, their destination, which rose abruptly from the ocean floor to five hundred feet where a lighthouse crowned its flat top.

Once or twice Irene made reference to the unspoilt beauty of the land, remarking pointedly that she was very thankful to notice that no developments were taking place here, and Carl, feeling unusually mellow and content, laughingly told her to shut up. She gave the most delightful giggle as she agreed to his request.

It was a day she was to remember for ever, for it stood out in all her memories as the turning point of her life—not because of the lazy hours spent driving to and from Stanley, or of watching with interest as Carl walked over the land where the houses were to be built and he planned the layout to get the best advantage of all the views. Occasionally he asked her opinion and when she tentatively said what she thought he gravely noted it in his book, remarking once or twice that it did help to have a woman's point of view at times.

It was on their return to Glendene just after dark when it all began. The room they always used in the evenings was in semi-darkness. Only one table lamp glowed in a corner and Mrs Marron was seated in her chair before a blazing fire, her white head bent and her long thin fingers gently caressing Lulu, who lay with sublime content across her rug-covered knees.

'Oh, you're up!' Irene gave a delighted cry as she opened the door and ran across the room to kneel beside her, looking up with a smile. 'How good to see you here again—are you feeling very much better?'

'Yes, thank you.' The words were expressionless and cold. 'Have you both had an enjoyable day?'

'It's been wonderful!' exclaimed the girl, and glanced over her shoulder with glowing eyes at the man standing on the opposite side of the fireplace. 'I've seen so much beauty that I feel slightly fey!'

Mrs Marron glanced from Irene's face to that of her nephew. He had a slight smile round his lips as he looked down at the kneeling figure, then his eyes met those of his aunt and his expression changed. Something had happened during the day which had wiped away her distress about Alex's romance.

'Carl, I want to speak to Irene—alone.' Now there was no concealing the iciness in her voice and Irene sank back on her heels, the joy fading from her face. 'Please leave us.'

For a moment or two he hesitated, wondering what this was all about. What else had transpired during the day? And in what way was the girl connected with it? His aunt continued to stare at him and without a word he went from the room, shutting the door very quietly behind him.

For a couple of minutes there was silence. Then Irene timidly put out her hand to touch the one resting on Lulu's fur. 'What's the matter?' she whispered. 'Oh, Mrs Marron, what's wrong?'

The other did not look at her; she moved her hand slightly and the girl's fingers touched the softness of the dog and then dropped to her lap.

'You remember I received a letter a few weeks ago, telling me of the decision to keep the gorge as a nature reserve?'

'Of course! You were so pleased and delighted.'

Irene raised her eyes and looked into the face above hers. 'Don't say they've changed their minds!' she added, almost in anguish at the thought of the beautiful, wild and lonely gorge being cleared and divided into building lots.

'No, they have not changed their minds about that project. But in the letter reference was made to other land and I remarked at the time that we need not bother about it for a while because it was a place which had not been mentioned publicly or in any discussions as a likely site.'

'I remember.'

'I had a phone call today,' the cold voice trembled with suppressed fury, 'telling me that ten acres of that land, which was to become part of a national park, has been purchased by a development company. Details were finalised last week and the transfer was signed two days ago.'

'Oh, no! How could they do such a thing?'

'Money can do almost anything these days. The price offered was such that the owner could not refuse.'

'But how did they know?' asked Irene in bewilderment. 'How did they find out?'

'There were very few people who did know about it. Perhaps three or four officials in the department concerned, apart from the Minister, and when he phoned me today, in great distress because he has the environment very much at heart, he was most emphatic that the leakage of information did not come from there.' The white head was lifted sharply.

'I knew because of my interest and the letter was sent from them to me in confidence. You knew because as my secretary you were entrusted with the acknowledgement.'

The girl slumped down on the rug, staring horrified into the stern face. 'Surely you don't think that I——' Her voice died away, for she could not put into words what she believed was being insinuated. 'You don't believe I had anything to do with it!'

'You read the letter, you knew to which part of the country it referred.'

'And you thought I passed on the information? But to whom?' There was no reply to this question, and determined to defend herself in every possible way from the accusation because she realised how much was at stake, Irene scrambled to her feet. She felt better able to cope when standing up instead of crouching on the rug. 'Mrs Marron, I told you once before I would never betray your confidence. What would I have to gain by doing such a thing, by telling anyone? Who could I have discussed it with? I knew no one connected with any development scheme who would be interested——' She stopped and drew in her breath. Mrs Marron watched the remaining colour fade from the youthful face and only just heard the one word which came from her white lips like a moan. 'Carl!'

'Precisely!'

They stared at each other. Irene did not lower her eyes, nor did she look conscience-stricken. 'I didn't mean what you evidently thought! I've never mentioned your work to him, I didn't know he had any connection with such things,' she cried, 'until we went to Tarrentall, and that was only three days ago. He told me then, and all that was said afterwards was of no consequence! Oh, don't you, won't you believe me?'

The twist of Mrs Marron's lips showed very clearly that she disbelieved this statement. 'You were speaking to a confederate of his, the day we went to the gorge for the first time. Neal Sheldon, the man I asked how he knew the meeting was to take place. He was with you for a while——'

'Only to ask who I was because he hadn't seen me before. Names were not mentioned by either of us.'

'Since then,' continued the other, 'you and Carl have become very friendly. He spends his evenings here with you instead of always going out as he used to do. He took you to Tarrentall, you've spent today with him, so don't tell me he hasn't discussed his plans with you and that you haven't talked about his work and your work.'

'I think you'd better ask Carl yourself what was discussed when we've been in each other's company,' was the very quiet dignified reply.

'I most certainly will. But not now. Only you could have done this, Irene, so I'm sorry, but I must ask you to leave Glendene tomorrow. I thought I'd found a perfect secretary, but you can't stay here when I feel I can't trust you.'

The girl was trembling from head to toe with dismay and indignation. 'And I couldn't stay, knowing you think me a liar! Oh, I'm so very sorry this has happened, but everything I've told you has been the truth.'

She rushed from the room, her eyes full of tears. In the hall she brushed past Carl, who was coming from the kitchen. He exclaimed, 'Hey, what's gotten into you?' but Irene did not answer as she ran to her room and let the door slam behind her as she flung herself on the bed, shaking with sobs.

Carl walked into the sitting-room where his aunt, her head up and her eyes closed, was stiff-backed and her fingers were clenching and unclenching on her lap. Lulu, unable to stand the grip of those fingers any longer, had jumped to the floor.

'What's happened to Irene to upset her?' he demanded to know without any preamble.

'I've told her to leave Glendene tomorrow.'

For fully a minute he was silent as he looked at her, then his face settled into the firm hard lines which gave him the impression of being so ruthless, remarked upon by his family at times and by his business associates quite often.

'What has she done?' his voice was crisp and demanding. 'You've been very happy with her and the work she's done for you.'

She smiled bitterly as she looked at him. 'The work she's done for *you*, you mean.'

'Stop beating about the bush, Aunt Kate. Tell me what's happened.'

So she told him, briefly and bluntly, and Carl went stiff as he listened. 'You can be ruthless when you want things to go your way,' she went on, 'or you can be as charming as Alex when he wants something. It depends on what you want and who you want it from. Wheedling secrets out of a young girl should have been easy for you. Even Netta has remarked upon your behaviour of late, staying here in the evenings, taking her out at night for a stroll in the garden, being pleasant to her and everyone else. She said you would be wanting *something*. I presume you flattered her and turned on all the Morgan charm, as your father used to do——'

'Cut that out!' he shouted, and then took a grip on himself, remembering she had been in bed for the past three days and that she looked very frail as a result.

'You did know about the transfer. It was your development company?' she asked.

'It was,' he admitted. 'But Irene was not the cause of me knowing. Believe it or not, your work has never been discussed between us. Conservation was mentioned once or twice and she defended your ideals, for she wholeheartedly supported them. In fact she took me to task for being on the opposite side, so to speak.'

'And when did she discover that fact?'

'On our way to Tarrentall. Either she was not interested before in what I did for a living or no one had bothered to tell her.'

There was a shrug of her shoulders. 'That's as may be. But if she didn't tell you who was responsible for the leakage of information? The day I received the letter we congratulated each other upon the success achieved and I watched her put it away in the folder with the other correspondence relating to the project and then it went into the filing cabinet. No one else knew. Just a few words, a sentence,' she murmured, 'and you would be astute enough to add them together and come up with the right answer. It's no use arguing or pleading with me, Carl, nothing will make me change my mind. I would never trust her again.' She passed her hand over her eyes. 'This last few days have been too much. Your mother, Alex and now you and Irene. Please ask Netta to come to me. I need her and want to go to bed.'

She wanted Netta's soothing hands, her affection which had never wavered in all the years they had known each other. Though she admitted that the housekeeper had faults, she wanted her gentle ministrations, and Carl, after giving her a hard look, went from the room. He watched with narrowed eyes as Netta wheeled the chair into the hall a few moments later before turning right and pausing outside Irene's door. She was still sobbing, and without bothering to knock he went into the room, looked at her shaking body and knelt beside the bed.

'Irene.'

She gave a gasp as she turned and saw his face on a level with her own. 'Did you tell her?' she demanded to know, nearly choking on a sob. 'Did you make her understand I didn't do anything, I

148

wouldn't ever betray either her or her confidences?'

'I know you wouldn't, in fact I know with certainty that you didn't,' he said comfortingly. 'But unfortunately, at this moment I couldn't convince her.'

'To be accused of such a thing! And I've got to leave here,' he winced at the despair in her voice. 'I must go in the morning.'

'So I was told. Now will you promise me something?' All the Morgan charm was definitely there as he looked at her and she nodded. 'Get undressed and get into bed. I'll bring you something to drink and something to make you sleep. Tomorrow hasn't yet come, who knows, by morning everything might be completely different.' He touched her wet cheek as he stood up and Irene closed her eyes, trying to make herself believe it was more than pity which was making him so considerate. 'I'll be back in about ten minutes.'

He had heard a car and knew Alex had returned from town. They met in the hall and Carl pushed his cousin into the room his aunt had left a short time before. Very briefly he explained what had happened, and Alex listened in dismay.

'But who could have given Twilight Constructions that information? There was only you who had any interest——'

'Yes, only me, but there was also Netta, who has such an interest in all we do!' said Carl with cold fury in his voice. 'Think back to the morning that letter arrived. We were all laughing at Irene and

Netta flicked the envelope across the table towards me, knowing I would guess who it was from and that it contained the decision of the powers-that-be—she knows so much of what goes on in this house! Aunt and Irene went into the study, and after reading it—and your mother told me this herself—Irene put it in a folder and then into the filing cabinet.' He hesitated and Alex waited in silence with bewilderment written plainly on his face. 'Later Netta was cleaning in there, the vacuum stopped suddenly and all went quiet, so I went in thinking something was wrong. You know you can hear her working all over the house.'

'Sure I know—even from outside you can hear her bustling round.'

'The letter was on the desk, prominently placed where I couldn't help but see it.'

'So you read it?'

'I did,' Carl nodded. 'Without even touching the thing.'

'And you passed on the information to your friends and they acted upon it.' His cousin turned away from him. 'Knowing what it would mean to my mother?'

'I admit it.'

'How could you do such a despicable thing?' There was scorn in the other's voice. 'Don't you earn enough from your own profession and from Tarrentall without having to help destroy the land you live in? You knew what it would mean to Mum, and now Irene has to take the blame for what you did.'

'I can't go in there and confess what happened without incriminating Netta. She must have gone through those files and deliberately left the letter where I could see it, she did what I *couldn't* and *wouldn't* do! You surely know why I can't tell your mother that Netta is the real culprit, even to clear Irene's name.' He put out his hand and swung Alex round to face him. 'Or would you rather I did tell her the truth?'

'No, no, you mustn't, you can't do that,' cried Alex with alarm. 'That would be the last straw. She needs Netta, no one else could take her place, for she depends upon her for so many things we can't help her with.' He bit his lower lip thoughtfully. 'I'm convinced something like this has happened before. She's managed somehow to get rid of all the other girls who've been here because she wants Mum to herself. She's jealous and possessive.' He wondered dismally what it would be like when Renate came to live at Glendene as his wife. 'She was furious too about the way Brutus spent so much of his time with Irene, who played with him and took him for walks. She needs cutting down to size, but for Mum's sake we can't do it. I can understand her motive, but that doesn't condone what you did.'

'Oh, I know.' Carl turned away impatiently. 'Look, Alex, this means I can't stay here either. I'll have to go home—I *want* to go home. Perhaps you can help——' he spoke rapidly for a few minutes

151

and the expression on his cousin's face changed from amazement to disbelief and his jaw seemed to drop.

'You wouldn't!' he cried.

'Ah yes, I would—and what's more, I will!'

'To hear you say something like that—it takes a lot of believing. But if you really mean it I'll go along with the idea. Providing Renate agrees.' He shook his head as though to clear it, still looking shocked.

'Good! Now can you give me something to make Irene sleep? One of those quick-acting tablets your mother has at times?'

A few minutes later Carl tapped on Irene's door and received a very subdued answer.

Carefully balancing the cup and saucer in one hand, he went in and she looked at him. Tears were still running down her cheeks and her hand as she reached for the cup was trembling.

'You're a very wet, bedraggled-looking little sparrow at the moment,' he murmured as he sat on the edge of the bed. 'Now take this with your first sip.'

Obediently she took the tablet and lifted the cup to her lips. 'Oh, Carl, where can I go, what can I do?' Her voice was quivering with emotion. 'I don't want to return to the old house and live with my brother and sister-in-law, and I couldn't go back to Sydney and live with Fran and Bill.' Not to the city again, nor to the small flat which, from Fran's ecstatic letters, had become, for some unknown reason, a fairyland castle filled with all her sister had ever wanted from life. 'I want to stay in Tasmania, so I'll have to go to Hobart or somewhere,' she whispered, 'and try to get another job. Will you help me?' she asked, forgetting at this moment that he was the cause of most of her distress.

'I most certainly will.' The cup was empty and he took it from her. Alex had said the tablet would work within minutes and he watched her closely.

'I'll have to have references,' she murmured. 'You asked for them, do you remember? Perhaps you'll give me one, for you know I've been diligent and thorough——'

'Yes, all those things,' he smiled. Her eyelids were becoming heavy. 'But you won't need them. Not where you're going.'

'Oh, am I going somewhere?' she asked very sleepily; her eyelids would not keep open. 'Where?'

He waited another minute before answering and then said quietly, 'To Tarrentall.'

CHAPTER 10

IRENE opened her eyes and wondered at the warmth on her face, discovering it came from a ray of sunshine, for she had forgotten to pull the curtains across the window last night. She could see the tree with the rosy apples and beyond that St Valentine's Peak standing out so clearly against the skyline, and for a moment she smiled at the lovely familiar surroundings. Then as memory returned she fell back against the pillows, remembering all that had happened a few hours ago. This was to be the last time she beheld this vista from her bedroom window. Today she was to leave Glendene and go over to Tarrentall.

Irene frowned. Had Carl really told her she was going over there? Had he been sitting on the edge of her bed, smiling, as he made this announcement? It must have been a dream, for there was something else she felt she ought to remember, and she sat up, hugging her knees and frowning with concentration, for whatever it was had some bearing on what had happened.

There was a knock and the door was flung open without ceremony. Netta stalked into the room and Irene could have sworn that there was a gleam of triumph in her eyes as she said,

'It's time you were up. Breakfast is ready for you

in the kitchen and Mrs Marron says will you pack your bags as soon as possible?'

'I intend to,' was the quiet reply. It was final then, she had to go, and as soon as the housekeeper had gone she felt the lump rising in her throat and the tears sting at the back of her eyes. 'But I won't give in again,' she thought defiantly. 'I won't let them see my world has fallen apart—unless the unbelievable did happen.'

As she dressed she wondered about it. If she went what was she to do at Tarrentall? Surely she would not be expected to live there alone? Thoughts and questions were spinning round in her head and she realised that the only way to find out precisely where she stood was to have breakfast, find Carl and ask, very tactfully, if he had happened to mention going over there. If he had not she would make some excuse for asking, explaining she had been in a daze after what had happened and no one, least of all Carl, would be allowed to guess at her loneliness as Glendene withdrew from sight behind the thicket hedge.

She was to have breakfast in the kitchen, which meant that the others had eaten, and after glancing at her watch she was not surprised. By now Alex would have finished at the kennels and would have left for his rounds and his surgery. Mrs Marron would be still in her room and Carl could be anywhere. Netta, uncompromising and taciturn, would be queening it over her domain; only Brutus would be there to look at her with trust and affection. She went along the hall and into the kitchen to find Carl standing by the huge oven, and when she walked in he turned to Netta and in the coldest voice either of them had ever heard him use he requested her to leave them alone. Netta stared at him suspiciously, wondering what he had to say to this girl, for he had been hanging about for the past half hour, getting in her way, she had had to walk round him and her few remarks had not been answered. So she flounced out of the room, not daring to defy the command in his voice.

'Sleep well?' he asked pleasantly, and the girl nodded. 'That tablet was strong, but Alex assured me it would mean restfulness and there would be no after-effects. He did confess he'd used it on cows and horses——' She laughed faintly at that information. 'It's all ready for you, and I'll have another cup of coffee while you're eating. Then,' he glanced at the door, 'we'll have a stroll outside.'

'Carl——'

'We'll talk later.' He glanced again at the door and Irene wondered rather hysterically whether if he went over and opened it quickly Netta would be found crouching on the floor with her ear to the keyhole. Something must have shown on her face, for he nodded and murmured, 'I'm glad you've caught on!'

She ate little. Even the lightly boiled eggs stuck in her throat and had to be washed down with coffee. Little was said, a comment about the weather from her, a remark about a new litter of puppies from him.

Ten minutes later they left the house. Irene paused on the top step and looked across the garden and the countryside, taking in its beauty and its peacefulness for the last time. As they walked through the orchard there was a scuffle behind them and Brutus, full of excitement as he held out a stick he had brought with him, joined them hopefully.

'You silly old thing!' Irene exclaimed with a catch in her voice as she took it from him and flung it as far as she could. Then she spun round. 'Last night——'

'Yes, it's last night I want to talk about. Everyone was very upset, you most of all, because you've been accused of doing something you didn't do.'

'So you believed me?'

He nodded and continued to walk beside her, staring ahead. He was silent for so long that Irene could not stand the uncertainty any longer and burst out— 'You said something to me after you'd given me that tablet to make me sleep. I thought I'd heard you correctly, but this morning, after thinking it over, I realise I must have been dreaming.'

'And what did you think I said?'

'You told me I was going to Tarrentall,' she stated baldly, and waited, holding her breath for his denial.

'You weren't dreaming, I did tell you that.' He picked up the stick Brutus had laid at his feet. 'When we were out there you suggested I return home, that I should take my friends and make the place come to life again. I replied that it might be possible if my mother returned. She's not coming back, so——' He flung the stick much further than she had done and Brutus went after it. 'I'm asking if you'll go out there to live and put into reality some of the plans and ideas which I guessed were buzzing round in your head as you went from room to room, pulling back the curtains and letting in the sunshine, looking so critically at everything. There was a wistfulness on your face when we left, because you did like it all, didn't you?'

She nodded, unable to speak as she wondered at his perception, and he glanced at her face. 'You liked the position of the house, the cattle and the horses, and you loved all the trees.'

'Yes, all those things,' she murmured, and did not appear to notice the stick which had been dropped at her feet, and the dog's wagging tail was an invitation for a continuance of this wonderful game.

'You don't want to leave Tasmania and return to the mainland to live with your sister and her husband, and I don't really think you want to go to Hobart or anywhere else. I want to go back to Tarrentall too, I want to live in my own home again.' He was suddenly at a loss for words and his lean face looked rather strained.

'You mean you want me to go there as a sort of housekeeper?' she suggested.

'No, I don't want you there as a housekeeper. I want you to go there as my wife. I'm asking you to marry me.' The words came out quickly in a kind of

158

jumble and the world seemed to spin around her as she closed her eyes. He saw her face go white and put out his hand to steady her. 'Have I shocked you? I'm sorry, but surely it's not such a dreadful idea? It isn't as if we've just met. We've come to know each other quite well. But if the thought of being my wife upsets you so much——'

'I'm n-not upset,' she stammered as the spinning stopped and she could focus her eyes again. 'Just s-surprised! *Very* s-surprised!'

'It's the first proposal I've ever made, and I seem to have made a mess of it!'

'Well, I didn't expect you to go down on your knees.' What on earth was she saying? 'I mean I didn't expect you saying anything like it at all. Why, Carl?'

'I thought we could both be satisfied with such a solution to our problems,' he went on trying to explain. 'We're out on a limb as regards a home, you have to leave here today and I can't stay any longer, for more reasons than one.' She felt once again, as he said that, that there was something she should remember. 'You liked Tarrentall, I've always loved it, no matter what you thought about my mercenary attitude, and I realised when I was there that the house would deteriorate if it's left much longer without attention. So much needs doing to it now. Decorum being what it is, even in this permissive society and especially in a place like this where everyone knows everyone else, the only thing to do would be to get married. We couldn't live there for years without the wagging of tongues, the pointing of fingers and the insinuations against our morals.' He sounded rather prim and Irene giggled, the giggle became a laugh and rather a hysterical one.

All she wanted from life was being offered her, not out of affection but because Carl wanted to return to his own home and she had not one to return to. She thought there might be some satisfaction being the mistress of Tarrentall, there might be more between them as time passed and they came to know each other better, or there might come a time —had she better put it this way?—when Carl would come to think of her in the same way as she thought of him. It would be worth the risk of trying. To have him there each day, sharing the comfort of their own home, knowing he was her husband and that they could depend upon each other, would surely recompense for other things. Around her would be the grey stone walls, the trees of Tarrentall, the garden and the paddocks. Once again she would be able to ride and they would drive together to visit friends who would in turn be entertained. In those things she could find happiness at the beginning.

Brutus was becoming annoyed. Nobody was taking any notice of him, so he jumped up at Irene with the stick in his mouth. The force of his great paws against her made her fall against Carl and his arms stopped her from being thrown backwards to the ground.

'Get down, you great brute!' he roared, and the labrador, with a most reproachful look in his eyes, stood on his own feet, his tail wagging slowly as he looked at them.

Irene allowed her body to relax in the strength of the encircling arms and once again felt the strange glow envelop her and inwardly she sighed. If only Carl had made this proposal with a declaration of love how she would have revelled in the closeness of him! She trembled, her own heart was thudding wildly and she realised he could feel it beneath his hand. He did, and looked down with anxiety in his eyes, thinking how small and fragile she was.

'He didn't hurt you? You're sure you're all right?'

'It wasn't his fault, he only wants to play as he always does when he comes out with me.' She made the excuse as she straightened up and Carl relaxed his hold on her. Brutus sat down, realising at last that no more sticks were to be thrown.

There was a strained silence, then Carl resumed the conversation where it had been broken off. His voice sounded hesitant. 'If what I've suggested doesn't appeal to you I'll take you to a motel in town until you've made up your mind what you want to do. But if you decide to go to Tarrentall we'll leave at once, as there'll be a lot to do and a great deal to sort out.'

It seemed a long time before she answered, for she was thinking that he was eight years older than she was, no flighty boy to be carried away by the events of the moment; he was a man who knew his own mind.

'If I go out there now what about the decorum

and the wagging tongues?' she asked, and he looked down into her eyes. The mischievous gleam was definitely there and he smiled in response to it.

'So you'll accept what I'm offering you? Tarrentall and me? We go together.' She nodded and his sigh was almost one of thankfulness. 'I promise you won't regret it. You would like a church wedding?' he asked very formally.

'Please.'

'As I have an idea we shall have to wait about three weeks in that case I'll ask Renate and the twins if they would come and stay out there until our wedding day.' How strange those words sounded! 'I'm sure she wouldn't mind, and tongues would be silenced by her presence out there. Alex will be able to drive over and see her and would help relieve any feeling of——' he fumbled for the word he wanted—'strangeness.'

'Unreality.' Irene spoke at the same time. 'It does sound unreal. Carl, are you sure you want it this way?'

'I wouldn't have asked you if I hadn't wanted you there.'

She wished she could read a different meaning to those words. 'And your mother, will she mind?'

'Why should she? She's married and living on the other side of the world. The house is mine and what I do with it is my concern only.' He looked at her thoughtfully, wanting to put her further at ease. 'I can even start a sub-division on the front lawn!'

It was a strange but happy day. Irene was humming to herself as she packed, and Netta, pausing outside the door, wondered why. Carl was on the phone for a long time and dearly she would have liked to have known to whom he was speaking. When she walked near he stopped talking and looked at her coolly; she could do nothing else but vanish out of sight and hearing.

The most difficult part was saying goodbye to Mrs Marron. Irene knew this would not be the last time they would meet; in time she would want to come to Tarrentall to see her nephew. She went to the bedside, expressing the fervent hope that the older woman was feeling better, adding that everything was up to date in the files and she hoped the stories about the penguin and the seal would be successful. Mrs Marron nearly broke her resolve to be distant in her farewell and looked at the girl, knowing she was going to miss her. Who would take her place? There were few who were so thorough and interested and she had been such good company. As Irene went through the bedroom door she nearly called her back to say she had changed her mind and she could stay after all.

Netta stood by the window and gave a running commentary on what was happening.

'It's Carl who's been waiting to drive her away! I wonder what the idea is?'

'Maybe I shall hear tomorrow that one of my friends in town has engaged her as a secretary.'

'It's to be hoped they don't make her a confidential one if they do.' She compressed her lips. 'That dog of mine is wanting to go as well. There, that's the last case in the boot. Brutus has been hugged, if you please, and the lass is getting into the car.' There was silence for a moment. 'Now she's gone!' There was no attempt at concealing the triumph in her voice and Mrs Marron glanced at her swiftly. 'Are you going to get up?'

'No. I prefer to be alone.' She turned on her pillows and shut her eyes.

'Just like that film star,' smiled the housekeeper with a happy chuckle as she left the room.

A stop was made in town at the surgery which was full of people holding pets of all descriptions, some with legs in plaster, others looking dull-eyed and sick. Carl went in alone and stayed only a couple of minutes, then Alex slipped out to smile at Irene and kiss her on the cheek.

'Congratulations! If it hadn't been for Renate I would have set my cap at you myself,' he said. 'She'll be out at Tarrentall this afternoon, plus twins, plus pups,' he added.

'And how did she know she would be wanted out there today?' enquired Irene.

The cousins exchanged glances. Alex said, 'Over to you, beloved,' and went back to his patients.

Irene glanced at the man beside her, waiting for an explanation. 'He and I had a long talk last night,' he said as they moved into the traffic. 'He knew I wanted to return home.'

'I sincerely hope it wasn't his suggestion that you asked me to marry you.'

'I don't need anyone's advice when it comes to choosing a wife!' he snapped between his teeth, and she reflected that it sounded almost as though he wanted her to marry him irrespective of Tarrentall. 'And I had to ask if he would mind Renate going out there—she was the only one I could think of at the time to act as chaperone.' Her lips twitched at that remark. 'I rang him this morning to say everything had worked out as I'd hoped and he went to see her.'

'What will happen when your aunt discovers that Renate, her sons and you and I are living under the same roof? Alex will naturally be a frequent visitor.' All the young ones would be together, and Mrs Marron would be with Netta, left to brood alone.

It was a forty-mile drive from Glendene, a drive through villages and narrow country lanes with views of the distant mountains. Carl promised to take her into the very heart of the island to see the many lakes and the highest peaks which were in wild inaccessible country and could only be seen from the distance on a fine day. There would be many places to explore and when the snows came they could go to the wonderland of the skiing slopes.

Mick and Ellis had not expected anyone to drive out to the house, least of all the owner of the place. They were sitting at ease on the portico in garden chairs and with their feet up, having their morning tea, when the car drew up, and Irene put her hand over her mouth as she watched their expressions change. Carl muttered under his breath as he got out and marched up the steps; he spoke only briefly, but within moments the chairs were being carried back to the garage where they belonged and the two men vanished out of sight behind the house.

Carl was smiling as he returned to the car. 'That fixed 'em!' he grinned with satisfaction. 'Taking advantage of my absence!' He saw the girl raise her eyebrows. 'Yes, I know I should have been out here before. But now I'm here things are going to be different. I own this place and I'm going to be boss.' Her eyebrows went up even higher and he laughed as he helped her out. 'You think that includes you too? Somehow I have a feeling you won't be bossed around.'

'Certainly not in the same manner as you boss the cowhands,' Irene retorted.

She walked into the house for the second time in her life and paused in the wide hall suddenly shy and very uncertain, looking at Carl with a question in her brown eyes.

'Go where you like, do what you want,' he said quietly. 'I'm going to get fires going in all the rooms —by now those two bludgers should have made some impression on the wood heap!'

Renate arrived about three o'clock with a car laden with food, something totally forgotten by the other two, who had had to share the men's lunches, clothing, two small boys, two small puppies and a budgerigar in a cage. Irene met her at the door, they looked at each other and in that moment a lifelong friendship was born. The little Austrian, only two years older than Alex, was exactly as Carl had described her, but had an enchanting air of maturity caused by having to plan for herself and her sons during the past two years. She had learnt dressmaking, so she could work at home and was very well-known in the district for her fine needlework.

The twins looked angelic as they waited, holding their puppies, for their mother to make the introductions, and waiting also for the inevitable remark about their appearance.

They were sturdy little boys and Irene glanced from one fair freckled face to the other, knowing if she called Walter she would surely be answered by Rudolf or vice versa.

'They have nicknames,' said Renate apologetically, 'to my regret, and I refuse to say them. But this is Australia, they nickname everything.'

'Shorty and Bluey,' Carl said them for her as he joined them. 'And don't ask me which is which. How are you, Renate? It's very good of you to come out here at such short notice.'

Her eyes twinkled as she handed him the birdcage. 'Alex, he say it is necessary for the good of Irene's name and owing to your reputation.'

'You might have informed me that you had one,' remarked Irene reproachfully over her shoulder, and the strangeness which had been there between them since their arrival disappeared with their laughter.

'It is very sudden, I offer my congratulations.' Gravely Renate shook their hands and asked anxiously, 'You do not mind the puppies? Alex, he gave them to the boys. The little bird is mine, so much easier to look after.'

Tarrentall began to come to life. Logs were burning in the wide grates in each room and the warmth from them began to creep through the house. After their first exploration, which was done in silence, the twins lost their shyness and became their normal selves, running up and down the hall, in and out of rooms, laughing at each other and at everyone else, and the pups were yapping and falling over themselves as they tried hard to keep up with the boys' twinkling feet.

Renate, who boasted unselfconsciously about her cooking, was busy in the kitchen; there was the sound of running water and the rattle of pans. Irene was moving between the bedrooms, opening cupboards as she searched for all she needed and airing sheets and blankets, and more than once Carl stood quite still with his head on one side, listening. He jumped nearly a foot into the air when the shrill ringing of the phone rang almost against his ear, he stared at it, snatched at the receiver and a voice said,

'Technician here, just testing.'

'How the devil did you know I would want it connecting again?' he demanded, and away in town the other man laughed.

'Alex called us and asked us to fix it,' he explained. 'Said you were taking up residence again, and as all the equipment was already installed we had only to make the connection here.'

'Many thanks.' So now Tarrentall was within

touch with the outside world.

It was starting to get dark when another car came down the drive. The twins heard it, looked at each other and raced to the front door.

'It's Mummy's My Dearest,' explained Walter as he cannoned into Irene coming out of one of the rooms.

Renate, her face a deep pink, came swiftly from the kitchen. 'They hear too much!' she laughed, and was halfway down the hall as Alex came in and the twins flung themselves into his arms. As their mother reached them he managed to enfold her within them too and the four of them clung together. Irene turned away, met Carl's eyes and they went into the lounge, where the puppies slept with exhaustion on the rug before the fire, and looked at each other.

'A great pity Aunt couldn't see them all,' commented Carl quietly, and Irene turned from him.

How she envied Renate having the privilege and assurance to be able to show her feelings so openly. There was nothing she wanted so much herself at the moment than to lay her own head against Carl's shoulder and feel his arms tighten round her with all a man's pride of possession, and she wondered how, in the weeks and months ahead, she would be able to conceal her feelings from him, realising how they would strengthen and deepen in the sharing of their daily activities.

CHAPTER 11

It was not very long before everyone in the district knew what was happening at Tarrentall. Mick and his mate had been in the habit of leaving in their old jalopy as soon as the day's milking was completed and they spent a great deal of their time at the club, so it seemed natural for them to comment on the fact that the boss was back on the property and would soon be marrying the little secretary from Glendene. Mrs Fursten and the twins were also out there, they added, and young Alex drove out every evening—quite a happy little family, said Mick, accepting another glass of beer with thanks. Oh yes, it was quite authentic, Ellis was telling other cronies at another table; Miss Peterson was wearing a ring with the largest emerald he had ever seen and she was already making alterations in the house.

So it was only a matter of time before the news was received at Glendene.

'So that's where Alex is spending his evenings!' stormed Netta after reporting the latest news received over the phone from their nearest neighbour. 'No wonder he never comes home until after midnight. And for Carl to marry *her*!'

'From the disapproval in your voice one might be pardoned for thinking Alex was your son and Carl your nephew,' remarked Mrs Marron quietly.

But it took more than a few words to put the housekeeper out of countenance. 'Well, don't you think it queer? I mean about Carl and the girl. Rumour has it they will be marrying within the next couple of weeks, wonder what all the rush is about?'

'You may leave me,' commanded Mrs Marron. 'I don't like your insinuations. Knowing both Carl and Irene, what you're implying would be the last thing *I* would think!'

Rather subdued, Netta left the room and scowled down at Brutus, who was always sulking these days. The dog, like the women, was on edge.

'Nothing seems to be in its right perspective,' Mrs Marron confided to her canine companion, and decided to wait for Alex. He saw the light in her room when he arrived home at half past twelve, having taken an hour to do the trip from Tarrentall, remembering the tone of Renate's voice as she clung to him when they said goodnight.

'Do not drive fast, my dearest.'

'Not more than a hundred miles an hour,' he had said jokingly, and felt her stiffen in his arms.

'Alex, you must not joke, it is not funny. Once before I have had a man come to my door to tell me. I could not bear it again, not when I love you so much—too much, I think.'

So, feeling righteous because he had done as requested, he tapped on the door of his mother's room and peeped in. 'Still awake?'

She nodded. 'I wanted to finish my book, it was an excellent thriller. Sit down for a moment, dear.'

Obediently he sat on the chair by her bedside. 'Is it true that Carl and Irene are enaged? And that they're to be married very soon?'

He did not hesitate. 'Yes, it's quite true. The date fixed is the twenty-fifth and the ceremony is to be at St Mark's.'

'And she's living at Tarrentall with Renate and the twins?'

He wondered how she had heard all these details. 'Renate is staying only until the wedding. Carl thought it best to have her there to stop any wagging tongues,' he explained lightly, hoping she would continue to use this mellow tone of voice. Then he might be able to say something about his own plans.

'Very wise of him,' she commented. 'I had no idea he thought of Irene in such a way.'

'It all came to a head when you sacked her,' he said quietly, and crossed his fingers as he added, 'Irene was so upset, he comforted her, and I suppose they discovered how much they felt about each other during the process.'

'I admit that I'm glad for his sake that Tarrentall is to become his home again, and I hope they'll both be happy. Is it to be a quiet wedding?'

He nodded. 'I'm the best man, old Mr Raynor who's been a friend of Aunt Helen's for years is to give Irene away and Renate will do whatever is necessary as regards the matron of honour or whatever it is.' He was rather vague about these finer points. 'Some of Carl's friends will naturally be there.'

'I would also like an invitation to be present,' said his mother softly, and he looked at her quickly.

'You want to bury the hatchet?' he asked with undisguised surprise.

'Carl is my nephew, and his mother would never forgive me if I was not there on such an occasion. Also, I was very fond of Irene.'

'Was?' he said softly.

'I still am,' she confessed. 'I've missed her very much, apart from the work she did for me it was pleasant to have such a happy girl around the house. I would like to see Carl before the wedding.'

'He's in Hobart at present and will be away a few days longer. That's one reason I've been going there every evening, to make sure all is well with them. But Irene has the reins in her hands—for apart from the house she's making sure Mick and Ellis do all that is expected of them, and believe it or not, they like her supervision and she has started riding again. Evidently she used to ride when she lived in the country before, and now she's up on Bacchus.'

'A drunken reveller!' interrupted his mother, laughing, and Alex knew there would not be a better time than this to explain what he and Renate had decided to do about their own future. No official engagement was to be announced until after the marriage of his cousin as they did not want to steal any limelight, it would only be a short one and then they would live either in her small house in town or at Glendene. Those were matters to be discussed later. And Mrs Marron nodded in silent agreement

173

and smiled as he kissed her goodnight.

She was no fool and in the hours she had spent alone since the abrupt departure of Irene and Carl she had been thinking a great deal, coming up with some unusual and unexpected answers. The only conclusion she could arrive at was to leave some things as they were and apologise for others. Netta would have to stay with her for as long as it was possible for her to do so, to send her from Glendene would be the end of too much, for no other woman would ever understand her so well, nor would she trust her person and her well-being to anyone else. Which meant she would have to close her eyes to the many faults the other possessed, including her dreadful jealousy. The large old stables could be renovated and rejuvenated, they could live there in comfort, a kind of Dower House, she thought drowsily, and Alex and his wife could live in the big house with the twins and which they would need if they were to have a large family, as he had confessed he hoped they would. On those thoughts she drifted off to sleep.

Irene's decision to ride Bacchus had been one of defiance. Carl had announced at breakfast one morning that he was driving to Hobart on business and he was sure they would be all right during his absence.

'How long will you be away?' she asked quickly.

'Maybe a week. I have a great deal of business to transact and might as well get it over and done with before settling down to life here. I don't want to have to go down again.'

She did not take kindly to the thought of him being away for so long when they were to be married in less than two weeks. While he was around the place and she could see him the whole idea felt to be feasible, if he was away she would think she had made it all up and the very thought of being without him now, even if he was not in love with her, filled her with panic.

'More development projects?' she asked tartly, and he nodded.

'You could call it that.'

It was then she remembered what had been tormenting her with its elusiveness ever since the day he had asked her to marry him and the realisation of what it meant hit her with the force of a brick being thrown at her head. She compressed her lips and surveyed him across the table with a look on her face he did not like or understand, and he turned to Renate.

'I think I'm marrying a shrew,' he remarked lightly.

'How nice!' she exclaimed, and knew immediately from his look of amusement that she had said the wrong thing. 'Shrew? I have the meaning wrong?'

'Yes, you have. It means,' he stood up, 'a cantankerous nagging woman,' and with that he walked from the room.

The two girls exchanged glances. Renate put her fingers to her lips but could not stop the laugh which bubbled from her throat. 'He teases you?'

'Of course!' Irene forced a smile and as soon as he had driven away she left the house and wandered alone round the wilderness which was the garden. But she was not looking at the weeds and the trees; she was thinking of the last night she had spent at Glendene when she had been so distraught. Carl had knelt beside the bed as she tried to explain that under no circumstances would she ever betray the confidence of her employer. Now for the first time she remembered the words clearly.

'I know you wouldn't, in fact I know with certainty that you didn't.'

No wonder he had wanted to return to Tarrentall! How could he stay with his aunt when he must have been the one responsible for passing on the information? There was no one else who could have done so, Alex was not interested and he would not go against his mother in an underhand manner. Netta was not interested either, her life began and ended at Glendene, and she probably had no idea what all the projects were about. Carl must have read the letter and promptly acted upon the information it contained.

She pressed her clenched hands against her mouth. No wonder he had asked her to marry him— his conscience, because she was to leave in disgrace, had prompted his proposal, added to the fact that he could not stay at the house after she had left. In the days they had been at Tarrentall his attitude had not altered in any respect. He was friendly, as he had always been, they had shared the laughter and the fun with the twins and he had taken her round the property and answered all her questions without any trace of impatience in his voice. Not once had he touched her in what could be called a lover-like manner. He had helped her in and out of the car, as he did Renate, once or twice he had lifted her from a chair or step-ladder as she took down curtains heavy with dust, with a laughing remark that though she might look like a little bird there was no need for her to try and fly like one as she would have to do if she slipped.

She paused by the gate and the brown horse lifted his head and came proudly towards her. Irene had not been forbidden to ride him. Carl had merely remarked one day that he would prefer her to wait until he purchased another, Alex would choose one more suitable for her diminutive size. At this moment there was nothing she wanted more than to ride, to race across those lush green fields as the Tasmanians called them, and over the fences, if she fell off and was trampled on or killed it would be no one's loss, she thought angrily. She wanted action, to do something she should not do, to make him as annoyed with her as she was with him.

Ellis was in the milking shed and in reply to her query said, 'Mick rode him a few days ago. Why, Miss Peterson, you interested?'

She nodded. 'I used to ride one just like him at home. Please saddle him.'

Both men had their doubts, Bacchus was fresh

and restless, but with Irene standing there watching impatiently Mick kept his thoughts to himself as he slipped the saddle over the broad brown back. They watched her swing herself up and tighten the reins, and as they moved away Ellis muttered something about her looking like a pea on a drum on that nag. Bacchus was only too willing to be off and Irene let him have his head and exhilaration replaced her annoyance as she discovered she still felt as much at home as she had always done when riding and turned towards a low gate, crying 'Up, boy, and over!' When the horse cleared it without effort she laughed and in the distance the two men exchanged glances and turned back to their work. There was no need for them to worry about the little lady.

Renate and Alex teased her without mercy during the first couple of days when she was saddle-sore and stiff and she took it in good part, for she had found a new interest which took her out of doors for a couple of hours alone. She felt she needed this and the relaxation to make her sleep instead of lying awake in the wide double bed in the room Carl's parents had used, staring at the ceiling, her mind full of doubts about the future. There were no doubts about her love for Carl, that had grown deeper since they came to Tarrentall; it was the wisdom of marrying him when he did not think of her with any great affection that kept her awake.

She was amusing herself jumping fences, not far from the garden of the house the afternoon Carl returned from Hobart, only two days before the date arranged for their marriage. He watched Bacchus clear the top rail with inches to spare, then his eyes narrowed as he saw who was on his back. It could only be Irene, wearing green slacks and a white pull-over, her hair blowing wildly about her face as she swung the horse round again for yet another jump. By the time they had cleared the obstacle, with a toss of the head from Bacchus, Carl was over the fence and walking towards them and as she reined in Irene saw the anger in his eyes and the tight set of his lips.

'Didn't I ask you not to ride him?' was his greeting. 'But to wait until I found something more suitable? He's too big and too wild for you to handle him.'

'No other horse could be more suitable,' she answered, leaning over and rubbing the nose of her mount. 'And I can handle him easily.'

'Why are you doing what I asked you not to do?'

She looked down at him, thinking it was nice to be able to do that for a change instead of always having to lift her head to look into his eyes. And there was no pleasure in them now, she noticed dismally, no delight in seeing her or of being home again, only annoyance that his wishes had been disregarded. This was the time for the showdown which would have to come sooner or later.

'Because I did not think it would really matter very much to you what I did. Not after what you did to me. It was you who passed on the information about that land, wasn't it?' Carl lowered his eyes.

'You did, didn't you?' she persisted, and he nodded his head slowly. 'Then you allowed me to take the blame.'

'Who told you? Alex?'

'You told me yourself,' and she repeated most of what he had said that fateful evening and the following morning in the orchard. Her voice rose. 'You and your developments! They ruined my friendship with your aunt, they lost me the job I loved. Why, you even threatened to subdivide part of Tarrentall!'

'That was a joke, and you took it as such at the time.' He grabbed the reins as Bacchus lifted his head.

'Then you went away and left me here, what have you been doing? Planning more subdivisions?'

'What have I been doing? I've sold all my shares and interests in the companies concerned and invested the money received in other things not connected with land, conservation or anything else.'

Irene stared at him. 'Why did you do that?' she asked in a whisper.

'Because I didn't want pointed remarks flung at me over the breakfast table for the rest of my life!' he cried vehemently. 'And if you're not satisfied about all those things and want to change your mind about what's going to take place on Thursday you'd better say so now. Before it's too late.' Never before had she heard such bitterness in his voice or seen his eyes look so tortured. That was the only word she could think of to describe them.

She did not move, she glanced down at him and then at the surrounding country and her reply was so softly spoken he hardly heard it. 'No, I don't want to change my mind.'

The reins were tugged and Bacchus was only too pleased to be off again, he took to his heels, cleared the gate and was guided towards the milking sheds.

Both of them were thankful for the presence of Renate, Alex and the twins that evening and Alex, noticing the way they avoided each other's eyes put it all down to pre-wedding nerves. He had brought with him an invitation for Carl to spend the last night as a single man at Glendene.

'Mum is a bit old-fashioned and thinks it's unlucky for the bride and groom to see each other on the day of the ceremony,' he explained.

'Aunt Kate is willing to forget what's happened?' Carl looked at him hopefully. 'If it pleases her, I'll go.'

'Yes, you may return, beloved, all is forgiven!' He smiled at Irene. 'Mum is going to the wedding too, so you'll see her there. And no doubt you'll see more of her later when you return from your honeymoon. Where are you going?' he asked guilelessly, and the affianced couple looked at each other with startled eyes. Honeymoons had not been mentioned during their short engagement.

'We're returning here,' said Carl quietly.

Alex looked disgusted. 'I intend taking Renate to New Zealand for *our* honeymoon,' he announced with an air of lordly pleasure.

181

'With the twins?' asked Irene.

'No, they'll be coming to stay with you at Tarrentall,' he answered calmly.

There was no time for riding, for spending a few minutes alone with Carl during the hours that were left. Irene had to go into town to pick up the ensemble she had made. Refusing to wear white with all the necessary trimmings, she had chosen a frock of deep cream silk trimmed with gold embroidery and a matching coat. She and Renate spent the rest of the afternoon at the hotel where the reception was to be held, supervising the placement of the cards of the guests, twenty in all, and planning the floral decorations, and throughout all the last-minute preparations Irene had the feeling she was doing this for someone else. On their return the twins had to be put to bed. They were naughty because they were excited; neither had been to a wedding before.

Carl left with Alex late in the evening. They all stood together in the doorway and he glanced down at the girl who would be his wife tomorrow afternoon. Alex watched him and then led Renate down the steps to say his goodnight in the shadows of the trees, a more romantic atmosphere than a doorway he murmured in her ear.

Carl's fingers touched the girl's hand. 'Don't be late,' he murmured. 'Tomorrow, I mean.' Then he was gone, blowing the horn loudly for Alex to join him.

Irene was getting into bed when the phone rang, by the time she reached the hall a white-faced

Renate was already there. The receiver was lifted and a voice said there was a personal call from Paris for either Mr Carl Morgan or Miss Irene Peterson.

'It's all right,' she whispered quickly to the trembling figure beside her. 'It's a call from overseas.' Renate smiled in relief and returned to her room.

Within half a minute a gay voice cried, 'It's your mother-in-law, or I will be that tomorrow, dear. I'm ringing to wish you all the happiness in the world for your future together.'

'Oh, Mrs Morgan, sorry, Lady——'

'Mother,' said the voice firmly and so clearly despite the thousands of miles between them. 'Is Carl there? Ah, I see! I would have rung tomorrow after your wedding, but about that time we'll be over the Atlantic somewhere—Honeybun has to make a business trip to New York. It's some God-forsaken hour here at the moment, but no matter; I like the sound of your voice! And are you as Carl described you?'

Irene laughed. 'Much depends on how he described me!'

'Small, petite, dainty, delightful and delicious!'

'Oh, you're joking!' She felt her heart miss a beat.

'No, dear, I am *not* joking. I know Carl, and if he described you in such a way then you must be *exactly* as he said. He wrote and told me you were all those things the day after he met you in Sydney; he said in his letter, and it gave me such a surprise, because I'd come to believe he would never marry and that I shouldn't have any grandchildren, that he had at last met the girl he intended to make his wife.' There was a silence. 'Are you still there, Irene?'

'Yes, yes!' Of course she was still here. She wanted to hear more of what Carl had told his mother, this woman with the gay light voice.

'So you can guess how delighted I was to hear from him that you had accepted his proposal. Poor dear, he wasn't his usual brisk self when he wrote then, for it read a bit *odd*, if you can understand me? Quite understandable, I suppose, for he said he couldn't believe his good fortune. Now tell me, truthfully and honestly, do you love him *very* much?'

'With all my heart,' answered Irene clearly, and Carl's mother heard something in her voice which completely satisfied her.

'I'm very thankful. He's my only chick and I want his happiness above all else. And Tarrentall? You like it? Good, good! Maybe Honeybun and I will make the trip——' there was the murmur of a man's voice in the background. 'Yes, perhaps next year, he says.'

She spoke for another ten minutes, admitting that the call was costing a fortune, but Honeybun could afford it and it was not every day her son was married. Finally she did say goodnight, and after sending her love and many messages to Carl put down the receiver. Irene stumbled back to her room, pulled back the curtains and looked out into the night where the trees were bathed in moonlight,

184

and with a deep sigh she laid her hot cheek against the cold glass of the window.

Mrs Marron thought it must be excitement, Alex could not put a name to what he saw in Irene's face and Renate thought how cold-blooded some people were not to show their feelings beforehand when they loved as Irene so obviously loved the man standing beside her at the altar. Carl's responses were firm and clear as though he intended the world to hear that he took this woman as his wife; Irene's were more subdued. She was in a daze which lasted through the ceremony and the reception, and it was not until they left for their car, for the drive back to Tarrentall alone, that she realised that it was all over and he was now her husband. She felt the warmth of his hand as they ran through the rose petals and confetti and remembered with a shock that he had kissed her for the first time in the vestry. So many had kissed her—Mrs Marron, now Aunt Kate, had done so with warmth and Alex with gusto. Renate had kissed her with almost sisterly affection.

Mick and Ellis had returned before them and acting under instructions from Alex had lit the fires and turned on all the lights; it was a welcoming sight to drive down towards the stone steps. It had been a quiet drive home; they had remarked upon various little things, but no mention was made of any personal feelings regarding the ceremony. The hall and lounge were filled with flowers and Carl raised his eyebrows when he saw them.

'They arrived this morning from town, ordered by my sister and brother and other friends,' she explained, taking off the small hat and shaking out her hair. 'Would you like a drink of tea? I'm longing for one, the wine made my throat so dry.'

He nodded and she went along the hall towards the kitchen; he followed and she hesitated for a moment as she watched him go further along to his own room. Her cheeks flushed scarlet and she shut the door behind her quickly, hoping he would not come in but return to the lounge and wait for her there.

The lights had been switched off and he was standing near the fireplace where the logs burned brightly and cheerfully. He took the tray from her, placing it on a side table, and turned her round to face him. The firelight shone on the gold embroidery at her throat and wrists and the heavy cream silk rustled slightly as she moved.

'My room is empty, all my belongings have been taken out of there.' There was a query in his voice and she turned from him to stare down into the fire. 'Did you think you had to—that I would insist——' his voice became husky and he added gently, 'There was no need to do that, Irene, I have no wish to spoil the friendship, shall I call it that, which exists between us now.'

She drew in a deep breath. How could she explain, how could she tell him? All the rehearsed speeches which had been thought over during the day, all she had planned to say had gone completely out of her head.

'Last night, after you'd left with Alex,' she said at last, 'your mother rang from Paris to wish us both happiness in the future. She sent her love and many messages, we talked for at least a quarter of an hour and during that time she told me of letters she had received from you after you first met me.'

'Oh, the scatterbrained chatterbox!'

'Yes, I agree.' Smiling as she turned to face him, she held out her hand and laid it on his; he glanced down at the two rings he had placed on her finger, the glowing emerald and the wide plain band of gold, and gripped it tightly in his own. 'She told me many things I wish you'd told me yourself, I would prefer to have heard them from you. She was very emphatic that you meant them. Did you? And if you did why didn't you tell me?' she asked softly.

'How I felt about you? How much I adored you? Because I wasn't at all sure how you would react to being told you were——'

'Small, petite, dainty, delightful and delicious?' Her brown eyes were sparkling. 'Am I really all those things?' she asked in wonder.

'To me you are. And much more, for from the moment I first saw you, looking so small and lost in the foyer of that motel, I was determined you were going to be mine one day.' He swept her into his arms and bent his head to kiss her, at first tenderly and then with growing passion. He slackened his hold suddenly. 'But you, darling, what about you?'

Her arms were round his neck and the glow she

had felt once before because of his nearness had become a fire running through her veins as he held her close.

'I moved all your belongings into my room this morning because I love you and need you,' she whispered in his ear. 'It was because of loving you so much that I consented to marry you—not because I was out of work,' there was tender laughter in her voice. 'Or because of Tarrentall, which I love so dearly too. Just simply because I wanted to be with you, whether you cared for me in the same way or not.'

'And all the time I was in Hobart I was thinking and planning the same thing! I felt so guilty about what I'd done to you and thought I would make amends by getting rid of all that had caused the trouble and which would have been a bone of contention between us. I wanted you here, to be able to see you each day, hoping that in time you might grow to love me a little.'

She sighed happily as she tucked her head under his chin. 'Not a little, Carl.'

'I can't kiss you when you're away down there,' he complained. 'And you needn't make yourself too comfortable,' he added as she nestled against him. 'Because we aren't staying here all night, are we?'

Irene lifted her head and what he saw in her face made him catch his breath as she answered, 'I hope not!'

A Treasury of Harlequin Romances!

Golden Harlequin Library

Many of the all time favorite Harlequin Romance Novels have not been available, until now, since the original printing. But now they are yours in an exquisitely bound, rich gold hardcover with royal blue imprint. Three complete unabridged novels in each volume. And the cost is so very low you'll be amazed!

Start your collection now. See reverse of this page for brief story outlines of the FIRST SIX volumes.

Golden Harlequin $1.95 per vol

Each Volume Contains 3 Complete
Harlequin Romances

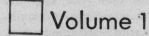

Volume 1

Volume 2

Golden Harlequin $1.95 per vol.

Each Volume Contains 3 Complete Harlequin Romances

Golden Harlequin $1.95 per vol

Each Volume Contains 3 Complete Harlequin Romances